Phil

Born in Warwick in 1948, Phil Street grew up in Kenilworth and Stratford-upon-Avon. He was educated at Kenilworth School - a fine school full of good teachers, one of whom ignited his love of literature and writing.

After finishing school, Phil joined *Flowers Brewery* in Stratford-upon-Avon where, for the first time, he tasted real beer - both illegally and for free. He soon realised though, that unlike a crystal ball, he couldn't see a future through the bottom of a beer glass. So, at the tender age of 17, he joined the GPO, which later became British Telecom. For thirty-three years, Phil worked for this great British Institution, retiring at the grand old age of 49.

Intending to play golf for the rest of his life, Phil quickly realised he could barely play at all, so taking the advice of a friendly neighbour in Banbury, where Phil lives with his wife, Mary, he went to work as a porter in the local general hospital. For the first time in his life, he received thanks every day from sick, frightened and vulnerable people, whom he was only too happy to help.

After finally retiring in 2015, Phil turned his hand to writing and to date he is still writing prolifically. This is his second novel - ***Murder Most Foul*** - based on a coach holiday to Skegness with his wife, Mary and four close friends, and a load of strangers.....

Follow Phil Street on his Amazon Author Page

Also by Phil Street

The Funboy3 Trilogy Series

Days Out.... A Catalogue of Ridiculous Yarns
Days Out.... More Ridiculous Yarns
Days Out.... Final Catalogue of Ridiculous Yarns

The Funboy3 Antidote Series

The Antidote To Brexit Boredom
The Antidote To Sense & Insensitivity
The Antidote To Normality

Novellas

Treading The Boards

Novels

Murder Most Foul

MURDER MOST FOUL

by

Phil Street

Warning: may contain some naughty words

Copyright © 2020 Phil Street

Phil Street has asserted his right under the Copyright, Designs and Patents Act, 1988 to be identified as the author of this work

This novel is a work of fiction. Names and characters are the product of the author's imagination, other than those clearly in the public domain, and any resemblance to actual persons, living or dead, is purely coincidental

Front Cover Image: Phil Street

ISBN: 9798561078354

Acknowledgements

I am indebted to Sheila Ware for all the help and time she has given to me and the patience she has shown in making sense of all that I have written and setting it down in a readable form.

I am also indebted to my lovely wife, Mary, for putting up with the fun, nonsense and stupidity that has lasted through every year of our life together. She is constantly reminding me of what the classical Greek philosopher, Socrates said at his trial for heresy:-
"The unexamined life is not worth living"

Preface

The power of choosing between good and evil is within the reach of us all so wrote Origen Adamatius an early Christian exegete and theologian the greatest genius the early church ever produced and who lived for the larger part of his life in Alexandria. Origen's views have been much echoed through the ages by writers such as Thomas Carlyle who said:- *"everywhere the human soul stands between a hemisphere of light and another of darkness."*

It is almost two years since my wife, Mary and I travelled with a group of close friends and forty-three other fellow holidaymakers on a holiday to the East Coast of England at Skegness and the surrounding area.

Those few days we all spent together would prove to be the most traumatic we were unfortunate enough to have ever experienced. What we endured during the period of our stay at the Loss Vagas Hotel Extra has left an indelible mark in our souls and something none of us are ever likely to forget.

The past is an unsolved mystery the present is a moving target
Edna Buchanan

Chapter 1

There could not be a more perfect day for a summer holiday to begin if we had asked for it.

Windless and warm, the sky without a cloud. The blue only obscured by a haze of light gold, as it sometimes is, in early summer. I couldn't think of many things more enjoyable than walking along a sandy beach. The sniff of a sea breeze, the shimmering colours stippling in the water or reflected from the fingers of wet sand. Who is not enchanted by the natural music of the waves as they rush noisily onto the shingle and between one's toes, only to creep back with faint lisping burbles into the bight.

Wooded hillsides are stately and river etched landscapes enticing, but they appear only like pictures when compared to the movement of the sea as it claws the shoreline. Even the breeze that shapes the tall grass or thunder clouds, which dress a mountain top, share no comparison. There can be few people who, after spending the summer by the sea, repress an ardent longing to make a return visit.

Technology is taking over, changing and transforming our lives and how we communicate with each other. However, over-dependence on devices such as smartphones, laptops and tablets can have a negative impact on our behaviour.

'Alexa, play Radio Four.'

"Here's BBC Radio Four.."

I knew I had said the wrong thing; I usually do. Everything becomes a problem when I open my mouth. It has this knack of getting me into trouble. I winced and pressed a finger into each ear while I waited for the inevitable.

'What the bloody hell is going on? Will you turn it down, for God's sake. What time is it ... I'm trying to get some bloody sleep,' the voice beside me moaned.

Does the response I received sound familiar? It might to some, it might to many but for me, it has become a daily ritual in our house; the moans, the groans and the protestations. Courtesy of Amazon Alexa, a virtual assistant, which stands on an old wooden blanket chest by the hammer attacking side of our bed - more of that later. At a simple verbal command, I can call up the Six o'clock News from the BBC, on the dot every morning, for a daily dose of cultural Marxism and personal opinion expressed as fact.

Having survived the hammer attack, I have always had the need to listen to the latest national and international news, to find out what had happened overnight and what was so different from the day before. Had the third world war started yet? If it had, who was winning. Had the BBC stopped banging on about Boris, Trump and Brexit? Surely not but more importantly, had a celebrity, minor or major, suddenly decided to escape our planet by kicking the bucket?

'I want to hear the news and find out what the weather is going to be like today,' I replied to the voice beside me.

'What's the time?'

Oh dear, she's not going to like this, I thought. 'Six o'clock,' I replied with some trepidation.

'Six o'clock! It's the middle of the bloody night,' barked the voice beside me.

"Over now to our political correspondent..."

'Oh for Christ's sake, Alexa. Play LBC London,' I shouted. 'I want facts, not bloody personal opinions.'

"LBC London... from Global player..."

'Are you going to make a cup of tea,' said the voice beside me.

By the way, the voice beside me, if you were in any doubt, is Mary, my lovely wife.

'I will in a minute. I would just like to hear first what the weather is going to do today. I don't fancy being stuck in that coach if it's going to be boiling bloody hot. Alexa ... what's the weather going to be like today?'

"This is what I found on the Web, In Banbury, it is currently eleven degrees. It is going to be cool and breezy for much of the UK today. There will be bright and sunny spells with temperatures in the high teens ... tonight, central and eastern areas of England will see patchy light rain. Otherwise, much of the UK will see clear spells overnight. It will be a rather warm night with the seasonal temperatures a little above average for this time of the year..."

'Alexa ... stop.'

The head beside me fought its way from the stale, sub-tropical thirty degree plus heat under the duvet, to the reality of the polar fresh eleven degrees above.

'What did she say?' queried Mary.

'It's going to pour down all day,' I replied.

'No she didn't.'

Aha, *She* was secretly listening, I thought to myself; no pretending otherwise. Mary was just as interested as me, to discover what the weather had in store for us.

'Where's my iPad? When you're downstairs, can you put my phone on charge, please.'

I managed to roll my way out of the bedclothes and sit on the edge of the bed. I did my usual shoulder roll with my arms outstretched and my hands trying to touch the ceiling. I experienced an involuntary intake of breath and yawned, a reaction to the tiredness I was still experiencing. I remembered back to when I was a child and mum would send me and my brother off to bed when we were wide awake and wake us up the following morning when we were fast asleep. Why was I getting up? I needed to; we both needed to.

Rolling out from under the bedclothes was the easy part as it happened. The more difficult part was to bend forward and try standing up.

'Bloody hell my knees ache,' I gasped. I find I have now started saying that every morning - signs of old age. I scratched myself in a couple of embarrassing places and performed a clothing re-adjustment in the most important of places where, I might add, I hide my crown jewels. Why are pyjama bottoms so bloody uncomfortable? You pay twenty quid for a pair and fifteen quid's worth gets jammed up your backside.

Some people prefer to sleep with nothing on at all - starkers, nuturellement nu - but I don't. The preferred side of the bed, on which I sleep, is very important to my lovely wife and decided upon by her. How thoughtful. If a burglar should decide to break in, then I would be the one to die first, she could possibly escape. Under these circumstances, perhaps sleeping with no clothes on, might not be such a bad idea after all. Confronting a hammer attacking burglar stark bloody naked, should he decide to strike, might have a damascene effect on the poor bugger. He might give up burgling and decide to lead a decent life. He might even decide to make an honest living - or like kittens.

Suddenly, a *"stop moaning, where's my cup of tea"* demand found its way from a face buried in a pillow. This is another part of my morning ritual, mashing tea.

After a few moments I managed to stand up. I was on my feet at last. A little shaky but I was upright. There followed an even more difficult operation, that of getting the tired old legs to operate correctly and in the right order and to make it downstairs into the kitchen without breaking either or both of them.

I managed to make it downstairs without injury but wishing as I did so that I had pulled a pair of socks on. The kitchen floor was absolutely freezing. Even worse, I managed to step on a small piece of grit that had, at some point in time, been stuck to the sole of someone's shoe. Bloody hell, it might as well have been a blooming great brick from a building site, it felt that large and sharp.

"Always run the water for a few minutes before you fill the kettle ... aerate the water" my mother used to say. I am not sure, whether or not, it makes an ounce - sorry, I forgot we are in the EU, 28.3495231 grams - of difference but I do it anyway. *"Don't be an MIF, don't you dare put the milk in first"* my wife is always reminding me. What can possibly go wrong, I think to myself. Well, apparently everything can, even though I know the recipe for making tea.

I chose a mug for myself, my favourite red one, and a 'Stechcol fine bone china made exclusively for Heath McCabe England Dishwasher proof cup' for my lady wife.

I was standing there, for what seemed an age, in my bare feet, with one of them damaged, and staring at the kettle. I know what you are all thinking and what you are asking yourselves - why? Well, the answer is quite simple and you must already know it. It takes a hell of a long time for a kettle to boil, especially when you are watching it. Silly question really, wasn't it? However, watching and waiting for the kettle to boil is worth the annoyance because it evidently tastes so much better in a 'Stechcol fine bone china cup made exclusively for Heath McCabe England Dishwasher proof cup', as my wife is constantly telling me ad nauseam.

Personally, I'm more inclined to believe the taste of a cup of tea is governed more by the blend of the tea leaf and the quality of the water in which you boil and steep it, and usually, I leave it for five minutes, rather than worry about the thing you drink it out of. I know I'm right but it's not something I would like to argue about, especially with my wife.

The first recorded instance of an Englishman drinking tea is in Samuel Pepys's diary and he wrote: *Afterwards I did send for a cup of tea, a China drink of which I never drank before.*

Okay, so it was a cup, and not a mug, but it probably wasn't a *Stechcol fine bone china made exclusively for Heath McCabe England Dishwasher proof cup.*

Now where was I? Ah yes, a Yorkshire teabag for me and a weak and wimpy alternative for Mary. And now for the, piece de resistance, soya milk. *"Don't drink cows milk, you'll end up getting cancer ... milk is for babies,"* my mother used to say. Was she right? Who knows, but as we have got older, Mary and I have taken to drinking soya milk.

The tea mashing ceremony was almost at an end, when suddenly I heard a shout coming from above. *"Sod off"* has become something of a ritual expletive at this time in the mornings.

There now followed the most difficult of all operations, that of making my way back upstairs carrying a man's mug and a *Stechol fine bone china made exclusively for Heath McCabe England Dishwasher proof cup* full of tea - Yorkshire in the one and a weak and wimpy apology in the other - without spilling a drop.

What on hell is he on about, I can hear you all thinking. What's so difficult about carrying two pots of tea upstairs. Well, in itself it's not a difficult operation atall, it's actually very easy, but the problem I have, and a personal one, is that my 29 inch - sorry, my 73.66cm - inside legs fit rather too easily and dangerously into the 31 inch - sorry, there I go again, my 78.74cm - inside legs of my pyjamas; the ones I'd adjusted earlier. Couple this with the distinct chance that they may, at any time and without warning, suddenly decide to drop to my ankles. Where is that burglar when you want to frighten him? However, as luck would have it, in this instance and on this morning, I made it safely up to the bedroom, thus avoiding death, destruction and embarrassment in the process.

'Where have you been? You've been ages. What have you been doing?'

'Oh, I'm really sorry,' I replied apologetically. 'I've been running the hoover around - incidentally, I have discovered that hoover is an anagram for husband - I've cleaned the car and the windows, dug the back garden and put the rubbish out. I have also put the world to rights and even popped round to our next door neighbour to put some lard on their cat's boil. Where the hell do you think I've been and what, pray, do you think I've been doing all this time? I've been making you a wimpy-washy apology for a cup of tea and, I might add, in a *Stechol fine bone china made exclusively for Heath McCabe England Dishwasher proof cup*; that is what I've been doing, my dear. Oh, and by the way, who was that on the phone?'

'Nobody.'

'Nobody ... you said sod off to nobody?'

'It was that bloody Amazon woman again. She was on about some membership I haven't got. She's bound to ring back in a bit so you can answer the phone next time and tell her to sod off.''

Mary was right, it was that very annoying *nobody*, who rings at least twice a day at various times and without warning, and it didn't take long for the phone to start ringing again and it was my turn to answer, just as Mary had predicted. I picked it up and before whoever it was on the other end could speak, I shouted *"sod off"*. How satisfying is that, I wonder. But no sooner had I put the handset down than it started ringing again. 'It's your turn this time, Mary. Give her what for ... there you are,' I said handing the phone to her.

It was worth going on holiday, I thought, if only to escape the bloody nuisance calls...*"Hello, is that Mister Streeeet? Vee have noticed a high level of... etc etc. This is Bli-tish-tel-e-com ... your in-ter-net connection will be terminated in fourteen days... We have been informed that you have been involved in an accident..."*. Oh really, that is remarkable; how did they know this and how did they know I'd come a purler on my tricycle and scraped my knees? They obviously didn't know my mummy had kissed them better. *"And, by the way, that was bloody years ago, so sod off!"* I remember shouting, and slamming down the handset. I wonder how many damaged handsets there are in the country?

'For God's sake will you sod off,' screamed Mary. 'By the way, Phil, did you find my earring stopper?'

'Earring stopper ... what the hell is one of those?' I asked raising my eyebrows questioningly.

'When I came to bed last night, I discovered that one of them was missing, it must have dropped off.'

'Where would I have found your earring stopper?'

'I thought you may have heard it being picked up in the hoover? You did say you put the hoover round, didn't you? I don't want a burglar breaking in and finding the house in a bloody mess while we're away.'

Chapter 2

A short while later, panic was starting to set in. Suddenly I was rushing around like a madman, wondering whether we would be late. I was sure of it, the coach will leave without us and all that money I had paid would be down the drain. Where the hell had I put our suitcase and holdall. Aha, a sudden brain wave ... why not ask Alexa, my virtual assistant?

'Alexa, where did I put the suitcase?' If I could find the suitcase then the holdall would be near it; more than likely inside. In fact, I was sure it was.

"This is what I found on the Web. A suitcase is a type of luggage. Suitcases are often flat, rectangular-shaped, with square corners. They are made out of either metal or..."

Alexa, stop!' Well, that didn't work ... maybe try again with a different question. 'Alexa, where did I hide our suitcase?'

"This is what I found on the Web. A nutcase is a fool or foolish person who keeps asking silly questions for which..."

'For God's sake Alexa, where is my bloody suitcase?'

"This is what I found on the Web. A soup tin is..."

'Alexa, stop right now.'

"A suitcase has been added to your shopping list."

Suddenly, it came to me. I remembered where I'd put it, and without the help of Alexa. I rushed into our small back bedroom, still in my adjusted and dangerous pyjamas, to pull the suitcase down from the top of the wardrobe, hopefully with the holdall inside; we would need both of them for our trip. I asked Mary to keep clear, to wait in our bedroom, while I dragged the suitcase down from its storage space between the top of the wardrobe and the ceiling. It wasn't because she'd be in the way, which of course she would be, but because she would be, as an asthmatic, in danger of breathing her last. I was completely wrong about the holdall, it wasn't inside at tall, but resting on the top. The bloody thing hit me on the head on its way down.

'Where's all that bloody dust come from? You're covered in it,' queried Mary as she started to cough and wheeze.

There was so much of it, it was difficult to see the colours of either the suitcase or the holdall.

'You'll need to pack an inhaler, just to be on the safe side,' I replied.

I didn't want her collapsing on the doorstep. As I said I had paid quite a lot of money for this holiday, and I might not get it back. There could be some clause in the microprint somewhere, which says that we must actually be on the holiday itself, and not packing a dusty suitcase and getting ready to go. What the large print gives, the small print takes away. It's harder to read than an optician's eye test chart, and that's with the correct strength of glasses.

Having heaved the suitcase, literally, into our bedroom, I dumped it on top of the bed and opened it up. Aah, so that was where I'd stored the Christmas decorations; I'd completely forgotten. I know it's only once a year, and it's great while it lasts, but setting up our artificial Christmas tree with all the decorations is a right balls ache. Though the grandkids like it, I suppose. Now came the question I'd been waiting for.

'I don't know what to wear,' said Mary in dismay. 'Will it be hot on the coach do you think? How long does it take to get there? Alexa, I don't know what to wear.'

"This is what I found on the Web. Try a trench coat with a pair of polished jeans for a classic everyday look."

'Bugger off, it's the middle of summer. Alexa, what should I wear?'

"This is what I found on the Web. A pair of your favourite cropped pants would be a good start."

'Bloody hell fires delight.'

'Look,' I replied. 'We're going to bloody Skegness, I would have thought a trench coat would be the perfect thing to take with you.'

'Don't be so bloody stupid, Phil. Why the hell would I need to wear a trench coat in Skegness?'

'The weather might be a clue there,' I replied. 'Ask Alexa again.'

'Alexa, what is the best thing to wear on a coach trip to Skegness?'

"I have added a trench coat to your shopping list."

'This is ridiculous, go with your instinct. Think about the possible changes in the weather. The East

Coast can be freezing at times, even in the summer,' I answered, getting a bit impatient.

'Yes, I know, but I want to look my best. I bet that Rose and Chris will want to look their best. They're always dolled up to the nines, with the pink lippy and that, when we go out with them.'

'Look, we're going to Skegness,' I repeated. 'We are not going to a fashion show. If Rose and Chris want to wear all those next to bugger all negligible looking things it's up to them. They could be arm wrestling you for your trench coat if the weather turns nasty. Ere, have you really got a pair of cropped pants?' I asked. 'I like the sound of them.'

'I'm seventy-years old ... what do you think I'd look like in a pair of cropped, bloody pants, for God's sake?'

'It was just a thought,' I replied meekly. 'Will you please hurry up as we haven't got much time. We'll have to leave shortly and I've still got the car to sort out. Alexa, what shall I have for breakfast?'

"This is what I found on the Web ... for breakfast, you can have banana vegan bread. The BBC recipe serves ten...."

'Alexa, stop. What can I have for breakfast?'

"This is what I found on the Web ... sometimes you can't beat a chicken kebab...."

Alexa, stop.'

"What would you like me to play? "

'Alexa STOP!'

"Okay ... I've added tomato soup to your shopping list."

'Alexa STOP. For God's sake, there must be something wrong with this stupid thing.' I shouted as I went into the kitchen and opened the fridge door but there was little in it, and nothing I could make a breakfast out of anyway. No eggs, just a drop of milk and no tomatoes.

'Have we got anything for our breakfast?' I shouted up the stairs. 'There's nothing in the fridge apart from a jar of olives and a part squeezed tube of tomato puree.' I'd told a lie, there was nothing in the fridge I fancied making breakfast out of.

'There's some bread and butter, some stewed apples and a jar of pickled onions. You could always make yourself some porridge.' Mary shouted back from the bedroom.

Bread? That must be the white block with green spots all over it.

'Have we any sugar?' I shouted up again.

'What do you want sugar for?'

'You said we'd got some porridge.'

'No, we haven't got any sugar ... use salt instead,' came the reply.

With no sugar to be had anywhere, porridge was definitely a no-no. Mary was right about the fridge contents, as it turned out. How could I have missed so many important breakfast ingredients. Buttered green spotted toast with stewed apple and pickled onions. I could top it off with an olive or two and a yummy squeeze of tomato puree. I was in the process of slamming the fridge door shut when I heard her coming down the stairs.

'Be a darling and bring my case down, will you, please,' she said as she walked into the kitchen. 'I'm all packed. Now where's that porridge? I hope you haven't eaten the bloody lot. And where's your suitcase ... have you already packed it? There's precious little time left before we need to get going ... we'll have to leave in a few minutes.'

In the time it had taken me to hunt for something - anything - to eat for breakfast, I'd completely forgotten about the time I'd wasted in my fruitless search. I dashed upstairs as fast as my seventy-year-old legs would allow and punched a few pairs of pants, some shirts and a pair of trousers into the dust-covered holdall along with my electric razor. I would find out later on that I'd forgotten the lead with which to charge the damn thing up.

'Have you seen my after-shag, I can't find it anywhere,' I shouted down.

'What ... that Dolce and Banana stuff?'

That's close enough, I thought. 'Yes, that's the one.'

My tin of Savauge. If it's good enough for Captain Jack Sparrow, then it's good enough for me, and if the television advert is anything to go by, then I too will soon be thrashing around on a sandy beach location just like Mr Johnny Depp himself.

'It's in my case,' called back Mary. 'I packed it by mistake. I thought it best to pack some protection. Can you put the Jungle Formula, in your case, then? I don't want to get bitten.'

I thought I'd have to remember that when it came

to dolling up and going out. I'd better not forget. I must not cover myself in Jungle Formula instead of my Dolce and Banana stuff, as Mary called it, so I decided not to pack it. We were not exactly going to the tropics, it wouldn't get that sticky.

'What the hell have you got in your suitcase; it weighs a ton. We're only going for a week, not twelve months.'

'Everything I have in the case is what I will be needing. You won't want me looking like a scruffbag, will you? You can dress up like a pox doctor's clerk if you like but I certainly am not. And besides, I have to make sure I don't double up with Rose and Chris as they shop at Marks and Sparks and Pri Mark as well. I'd die of embarrassment.'

I had completely forgotten the time when we all turned up at a disco night out together. Rose and Chris were wearing identical David Essex Fan Club tank tops.

'I struggled to fit your tin of Tart Spray in my case, and for heavens sake hurry up,' she shouted.

Oh, so it was my fault her suitcase was heavy enough to sink the bloody Bismarck. Yet another fault to add to the long list of faults that all men seem to have. Everything we say and everything we do.

Fortunately, I managed to avoid a hernia, lugging the damn suitcase downstairs and scraping it along the hall carpet to the front door. It was time to leave. Alan and Rose had said I could park my car at their place, and then we could share a taxi to the bus stop, by the side of the De Montfort Hotel at Abbey End in

Kenilworth, where we would await the coach.

'Alexa, where did I put my car keys?'

"Sorry, I'm not sure."

'Oh no. Alexa, where are my bloody car keys?'

"This is what I found on the Web ... the large...."

'Alexa STOP, for Christ's sake. Alexa, where are my friggin car keys?'

"I have added a copy of a copy of the Bible to your shopping list."

'Alexa, for heavens sake, STOP.'

Chapter 3

'By the way, where are we going?' enquired Mary. 'You haven't told me yet ... you said it was a surprise.'

Surprise, did I actually say that, I thought to myself. I suppose I must have done but I don't remember using the word *shock*.

'We're going to Skeggie,' I replied with some trepidation. 'I thought I told you earlier? In fact, I know I did.'

Blimey, that certainly was a conversation stopper. I think Mary was both surprised and shocked, a double whammy. I don't know what she had conjured up in her mind; a romantic week away, perhaps? She had probably asked Alexa? Had Alexa said to her - *"this is what I found on the Web ... you can expect an infinity pool and a candlelit dinner...."*. Were pillowcases and fluffy towels, folded into the shape of cuddly swans, mentioned, I wonder. *"There will be pillowcases and fluffy towels folded into the shape of cuddly swans...."*

'Didn't you ask Alexa, then?'

'I did,' she replied. 'She told me, *"I have added trench coat to your shopping list"*. You know what, I'm going to send that bloody thing back. Has Alexa got ESP or something, or is it that whenever you mention going on holiday in England, a trench coat is always seen as an essential item of clothing?'

'What ... the trench coat or Alexa?' I queried.

'Skegness, I thought you were joking. Skegness is a bloody dump. Ere, I hope we're not stopping in a bloody caravan ... we aren't, are we? Not Butlins is it? Surely this is some sort of a bloody joke ... turn the car round now ... we are not going ... I'll never live it down,' retorted Mary, getting her knickers in a twist.

'Look,' I replied. 'You can tell a few little white lies when we get back. Just tell your friends you've been to Tenerife or Majorca or somewhere else, anywhere. They'll believe you, they won't be any the wiser.'

'What, like where haven't I not got the bloody suntan from?'

'Just say it was cloudy all the time you were there. Ere, you haven't packed some skimpy swimsuits, have you? You ain't thinking of going topless? Incidentally, I fancied poached eggs on toast for breakfast this morning but there weren't any eggs.'

'You wish. They'll be expecting me to bring them back one of those Spanish hats or a bloody great donkey with all those dangerous spiked things stuck in it ... you know, that holds its head on.'

'Tell them you fell asleep on the beach and the shop was closed when you finally managed to get there ... you know them, they'll believe anything you say.'

Butlins, blimey, that brought back some memories. I could just picture Billy and a red-coated army marching south from Filey, back in 1945, and taking the camp he'd opened in 1936, back from the Navy after World War Two.

'No, it's not Butlins and it's not a caravan either,' I replied reassuringly. 'So keep your wig on, for God's sake. According to what I've been told, Skeggie is a place of extraordinary beauty, and unrivalled in the United Kingdom. A mate of mine was there recently he told me it's on the list to become a UNESCO World Heritage site ... said it exerts magnetism, and is an architectural showcase for the world. It catches the dynamism of modern everyday life, and it's also a sandwich cake of fossilisation, to which someone has taken a juicer. A mix of styles, and an experience practically unrivalled anywhere else in Lincolnshire. You know what he said to me - *"If I were good at painting then I'd paint this".*'

Actually, I really said - okay mate, that's what the guide books say, but what's it really like, what's your honest opinion, but I hadn't the courage or heart to tell Mary his reply was, it was indeed a dump. It would appear that there are lies, damn lies, and Skegness visitors guide books.

'Didn't that John Betyerman bloke write a poem about dropping bombs on it ... said it was no use to any bugger anymore,' stated Mary, thoughtfully.

'No, you idiot, that was Slough, and it was John Betjeman, not John Betyerman.'

Perhaps the German bombers couldn't find it on *Die Landkarte* because they hadn't flown that far north? It's either that, or if they had and they saw it from above, then they probably thought the holiday camp would have looked like a perfect ready-built prisoner of war camp, in the event of Adolf Hitler's, Operation Sea Lion, invasion being successful. Who knows - God must have been having a great day when he saved Skegness from the - Hermann the German's - bombs.

The drive across to Kenilworth had been quiet enough, the roads were clear and there was hardly any traffic at all. Mary sat there quietly in the passenger seat, but staring straight ahead for most of the entire forty-five-minute journey to Alan and Rose's, where I was to park our car. Whatever was troubling her could soon be landing in my lap, and troubling me; I could just sense it.

'Come on you two, you're late,' said Alan. 'The coach picks us up at eight o'clock. Where have you been?'

Alan and Rose were standing there waiting for us as we pulled into the parking area, opposite their first floor flat in Kenilworth.

'The taxi will be here any second now. Rose, help Mary get her suitcase out of the car ... don't let her struggle on her own,' instructed Alan.

'Why don't you help her, you lazy git. You're supposed to be the one with the muscles.'

Muscles? Alan with muscles? I couldn't say they were much in evidence unless, of course, they'd journeyed southward and were stopped from reaching the south pole by the belt on his trousers?

'Come here ... let me have a go, then,' he answered shortly. 'Don't blame me, though, if I have one of my spasms. You'll have to keep your hands to yourself. Jesus, Mary, what in the hell have you got in this case ... it weighs a bloody ton. We're only going away for a week, you know.'

'I've got my make-up...'

'Blimey ... have you got anything else in there, like clothes?' chortled Alan.

'Did you hear what he just said, Phil? Are you going to stand for that?' retorted Mary indignantly.

'Well, did you pack some clothes as well?' I queried.

'Of course, I've packed some bloody clothes, you cheeky swine. I knew I shouldn't have come. This week is going to be a bloody disaster ... I can feel it in my water.'

'By the way, Alan ... can I use your toilet, mate?' I asked. 'I'm busting for a wee.'

I had just flushed the toilet, and was barely halfway down the stairs, when I heard the taxi pulling up outside. I heard Alan say morning to the driver as I stepped through their front door, pulling it shut behind me.

'Alan, give the driver a hand with the cases,' ordered Rose.

'That's okay ... you climb in folks, and I'll do the business with the cases,' replied our friendly driver as he opened the lid of the boot and asked us where we were going. 'Let's pray the weather's kind. Hope you've packed a trench coat; you might need one later on in the week. Apparently, it's going to chuck it down on Friday.'

It was a bit of a tight squeeze in the taxi but we all managed to fit in. Mary, Rose and Alan squeezed into the back and I jumped into the passenger seat beside the driver. I had just belted myself in when I heard a moan coming from behind me.

'What the bleedin hell ... who the ... Jesus Christ what have....'

I looked over my shoulder. 'Mary, it's that bloody suitcase of yours. The poor bugger's probably squeezed his large colon out lifting the bloody thing into the boot.'

'Is that the one with the make-up in?' enquired Alan. 'Do you need a hand, mate?' he shouted to the driver, who appeared to be struggling at the back of the car. 'If you do, my missus is here to help, ain't you sweetheart.'

'No ... I'm okay ... nearly there,' came the reply from the driver as he slammed the boot lid down with a thud and a blast of air pushed its way to the front of the car.

'Are you alright mate?' I enquired, as the driver opened his door and climbed in. 'Sorry about the heavy suitcase, it's not mine by the way. You should have asked for help. Rose would have helped, wouldn't you Rose?'

At last we were off; our holiday had begun. We were on our way to the sunny east coast town of Skegness for some fun, sea, sand and frolics.

'Bloody hell, what's that smell. Ere you haven't apple-tarted, Alan?' I asked holding my nose.

'Of course I haven't, you cheeky sod. A dirty dog

smells his own smells first ... it must be you, mate.'

'It certainly isn't me. You'd all be dead by now. Here girls, it's not, by any chance, one of you ... is it?'

I was just about to receive an angry answer when the taxi driver chipped in and owned up. 'Sorry everyone, it's me.'

'What, it's you who's backfired then, driver?' Rose asked, screwing her face up.

'No, I haven't farted ... I trod in a bloody dog banger outside your flat,' he replied crossly. 'The ground is covered with them. It's not your dog, is it? Why don't you pick up the bloody crap and bag it ... it's all over my bloody shoe. I've got to live with this for the rest of the bloody day. My missus will go barmy when I get home ... she won't let me in the bleedin house.'

'Sorry, mate. We ain't got a dog but the bloke in the flat below us has,' replied Rose. 'Bloody dirty things. They ain't got no responsibilities. You shove the food in one end and they don't give a monkey's where it fires out at the other. I looked out the flat window last night and saw this thing crapping on the car park. It must have been what you've just trodden in. I thought a kangaroo had escaped from a zoo somewhere until I heard the idiot below shouting to Eric to come in.

'Eric ... who the hell is Eric?' piped up Mary.

'Eric is the name of this bloke's greyhound. It's a bloody great thing. Can't understand why he wants one of those things for.'

'If I might change the subject,' I butted in. 'Where

is the coach picking up Mick and Christine?'

'At the coach station in Digbeth, but we've got a pick up in Coventry first, outside the swimming baths,' replied Alan.

Good, I thought to myself, it won't take too long to get there. We were dropped off at the bus stop outside the De Montford Hotel in Abbey End as planned. There were already four other people waiting with their suitcases. I assumed rightly that they were going on the same holiday as us.

After unloading the suitcases, the taxi driver seemed to stand around for a while, looking in Alan's direction, and issuing a cough or two. Whatever he was waiting for, he eventually gave up and stormed off in some sort of a huff.

'What was that all about, Alan?' I asked.

'He was hanging about for a tip.'

'Did you give him one then ... how much? What do I owe you?'

'I gave him a tip all right ... told him that next time to make sure to have a load of wet wipes in his cab. The bloody smell was terrible, but he wasn't happy.'

I did not recognise any of the four people who were already there at the bus stop, and nor did Alan or Rose. It transpired they'd travelled from Leamington to pick up the coach. However, one thing I did notice was one of the ladies appeared to be sobbing. Had she also discovered, like Mary, that a romantic week away with her loving husband, whom I'd heard her call Barry, was a trip to Skegness? That there would be no infinity pool or fluffy towels folded into the shape of cuddly swans?

'Don't worry,' I said. 'You'll love it when you get there. I only wish my mum and dad were here to go with us.'

At this, the woman burst into a flood of tears, sobbing her heart out she was. Blimey, surely Skegness ain't that bad, I thought to myself. I imagine it's a bit loud and rough around the edges but not bad enough to cause so much disappointment and so many tears.

'Sorry,' was it something I said?'

Her husband, Barry was quick to jump in and apologise. 'No mate, no need to apologise ... it was nothing really. It was when you mentioned your mum and dad, that's what got her going. We nearly didn't come because Shirley lost her mum a couple of days ago, and she's finding it difficult to come to terms with it. To make matters worse, when she went back to WH Smiths to get her money back on a get well card, they wouldn't give it to her.'

'Why was that ... bloody hell that's a bit heartless, isn't it,' I said.

'She could have swapped it for a bereavement card instead,' piped up Rose.

'Yes, I did think that at the time but she'd already written her mum's name in it.'

'So what!' exclaimed Alan. 'Surely, someone else could have bought it, if their mum had the same name. What was Shirley's mum's name?'

'Jocasta,' replied Barry, the sobbing woman's husband.

They could wait a long time to resell that one, that is if they could sell it atall, I thought, smiling to myself.

'Oh dear, I know exactly how she feels,' said Rose sympathetically.

'Why's that ... have you lost your mum recently?' enquired Barry.'

'No, not my mum, she died bloody years ago, bless her. No, I lost a winning scratch card. Searched everywhere for it, didn't we Alan. I'd won five quid on it, and I was distraught, wasn't I?' replied Rose, turning to look at Alan.

'That she was. I couldn't do anything with her. Bawled her eyes out for days, didn't yer duck.'

'I certainly did.'

'What on earth is that?' Mary asked.

'I have no idea,' I replied, looking around.

Mary had drawn my attention to something she had seen approaching us, along the Warwick Road. Whatever it was, it was making a very strange noise and enveloped in a cloud of black smoke. It took me a while to decide that, in fact, it was a coach, our coach, which was coming to pick us all up and take us to Skegness. There was a grinding noise as it came to a halt at the bus stop, where we were waiting, by the side of the De Montfort Hotel.

'Is this it, a luxury coach?' queried Rose, looking aghast. 'They're avin a tin bath, ain't they? A luxury coach ... surely not, it's a bloody rust bucket. It's one MOT away from a bloody junkyard. In fact, that's probably where they bought it.'

I looked at the driver, who appeared to be searching for neutral in the coach's gearbox, by waving the gear lever from side to side. Finally, he found what he was searching for, pulled the handbrake on and stepped from the coach.

'I have a Mr and Mrs Sleet, a Mr and Mrs Gay, a Mr and Mrs Grump and a Mr and Mrs Snotgrass for the Skegness trip,' he read off as he traced a finger down a list attached to his clipboard.

We were so tired as the result of having to get up so early, that we were not inclined to query the information the driver had been given. We knew we were the passengers on his list and so acknowledged his query, that we were indeed, who he was expecting to pick up. Climbing aboard as requested, we made our way to our allocated seats. Mary and I were in 27 and 28 and Mr and Mrs Gay, Alan and Rose, were in 23 and 24.

Finally, with our suitcases safely stowed away in the baggage compartment by the driver, he climbed into the seat behind the steering wheel and searched for the right gear, crunching into the right one by chance and then we were off, leaving a cloud of smoke billowing behind.

Chapter 4

Voted one of the coolest neighbourhoods in Britain by a national daily newspaper, Digbeth is just a short walk from Birmingham City Centre, and it was here that our coach struggled into the main National Express coach station. As we crept into the bus station I noticed, that on the side of a building, there was a large sign, which read *A Hundred Thousand Welcomes*. I saw our friends, Mick and Chris, climbing out of a taxi, which they had taken from their home in Shard End. After grinding to a halt, the driver applied the handbrake, and then climbed out of his seat, and stepping through the coach's entrance door, he shouted, 'Any passengers for Skegness.'

'That's us, mate,' shouted a voice.

'Is it Mr & Mrs Swiney?' enquired the coach driver.

'No, mate, it's Sweeney.'

'It's not you, then. I'm waiting for Michael and Christine Swiney.'

'That's us. We're Michael and Christine.'

'I thought you said your name was Sweeney?'

'It is ... you must have been given the wrong name,' replied Mick.

'Oh ... right ... I see. Okay then, welcome aboard Mr and Mrs Swiney-Sweeney.'

'It's Mr and Mrs Sweeney ... not Swiney-Sweeney,'

'Michael and Christine, is it?'

'Yes, mate.'

'Our cases are over there,' Mick shouted to the driver as he and Christine climbed aboard.

I heard the bus driver telling Mick and Chris he would take care of their cases. 'Your in seats 25 and 26, in the middle by the steps to the emergency exit and toilet.'

Who the hell it had been on the other end of the telephone, when I booked the holiday, God only knows. Whoever it was, they were either deaf or couldn't spell? Mick and Chris were down as the Swineys; Alan and Rose were the Gays, instead of Day and Mary and I were now Mr and Mrs Sleet. Goodness knows who the Grumps and the Snotgrass were supposed to be.

We would find out later that Grump and Snotgrass were the only names, which the someone, on the other end of the telephone, managed to get right, and spell correctly.

Suddenly the side panels of the coach covering the baggage area moved upwards and the next thing I heard was the driver moaning.

'Bloody hell, fire's delight,' he exclaimed. 'What the hell have they got in this bleedin case? If I take a corner too quickly, the bleedin coach will slew off the bleedin road.'

'Sorry, mate,' shouted Mick. 'That's the wife's.'

Mick and Chris slowly wended their way along the coach, introducing themselves as they went, with a *good morning* or an *all right our kid,* to anyone who looked up until they reached their seats in the middle. What happened next was amusing to some passengers, but very irritating to others.

'You didn't tell me, Mick, that we were going to Skegness,' huffed Chris.

'I did, so,' replied Mick indignantly.

'No, you damn well didn't.'

'I'm sure I did.'

'Well, I can assure you, you didn't. God almighty it's a dump.'

'No, it isn't.'

'Yes, it bloody well is. Anyway, it's my turn to sit by the window.'

'No, it's not. You sat by the window last time.'

'No, I didn't.'

'Yes, you did. Remember, when we went to Weymouth,' said Mick getting quite angry and exasperated.

'Weymouth? I don't remember that.'

'I do. You nearly had a fight with that woman you insulted. I'm surprised her husband didn't stick one on you. I wouldn't have been able to protect you with my bad arm.'

'Insulted what woman?' queried Chris.

'You remember? You asked her if she was wearing a wig, and if her teeth were her own. I remember you saying, *"I don't want to appear ageist but...."*. What a thing to say to the poor woman.'

'Oh, her. That wasn't her husband, he was a bloody toy boy. He must have been at least twenty years younger with all that bum-fluff on his chin. I do remember, now you've mentioned it. I was right though, wasn't I? She forgot to pop her teeth in, when we went on a day out to that Lulworth Cove place, and ended up in a pub because it was pissing down with rain. Disgusting, she was, sucking on that pork sausage ... I ask you. Everyone was gawping at her. and some poor bloke got his head slapped because he couldn't take his eyes off her. All that dribbling, it was enough to put me off a runny egg. And she took off her hair to fan her face when she had a hot flush. By the way, that wasn't the last time I sat by the window ... that was the time before. I didn't sit by the window last time, you did, and you always sit by the window when we're out in the car.'

'That's because I drive the bloody thing, that's why I sit by the window. You sit by the window as well, on the passenger side.'

'No, I never sat by the window last time.'

'Yes, you did.'

'No, I didn't.'

'Where were you then?'

'At home ... watching *Strictly*.'

'So was I, then.'

'No, you weren't.'

'Yes, I bloody well was.'

'Did you see that Craig Gravel-Hardboard bloke give that Debbie McGee a ten, then?'

'No. I don't remember him giving any bugger a

ten out of ten. Why?'

'Well, there you are then. That's because you were sat by the window.'

'How do you mean, sat by the window? I sit in an armchair, next to the door into the bloody lounge. What the hell are you on about?'.

'No, you weren't.'

'Where was I then, for God's sake?'

'You were sat by the window.'

'Sat by the window, where?'

'You were sat by the window in the car. You went out to pick up a pizza.'

Suddenly there was a loud eardrum bursting squeal and shouts of, *"Jesus what the bloody hell..."* from a few of the passengers.

'Sorry folks,' said our driver, as he stood up and tapped the end of the microphone to test the sound system. 'One-two, one-two ... ladies and gents ... could I have your attention, please? Can Mr and Mrs Swiney-Sweeney sort themselves out and decide who is going to sit where? Can they please sit themselves down so we can get going ... thank you.'

'Always causing trouble, you are,' Chris whispered in rather a loud voice.

'Who ... me?' replied Mick.

'Yes, you. You did it the last time.'

'No, I didn't.'

'Yes, you did. I remember that bloke took a swing at you. Telling him he didn't know what the hell he was talking about, and calling him a thicko.'

'Well, he was, wasn't he?'

'Wasn't he what?'

'Thick. Everyone knows the Atlantic Ocean is saltier than the Indian.'

'How the hell do you know which bloody ocean is saltier?'

'My mate, Paddy, told me ... and he doesn't tell lies.'

'Yes, he does.'

'No, he doesn't,' repeated Mick emphatically.

'Yes, he does. Everyone knows the Pacific Ocean is the saltiest. I've a good mind to go back home right now,' Chris retorted angrily.

The couple who were sitting directly behind Mick and Chris and been listening in to what they were arguing about leaned forward and said. 'Sorry to interrupt, but is it not the North Sea, which is saltier?'

Mick and Chris turned and looked at one another, and then over their shoulders to the couple behind, and in unison said, 'No.'

Suddenly, there was another ear-shattering squeal on the coach's intercom, followed by a tapping on the microphone by the driver.

'One-two, one-two ... ladies and gents. I have some bottled water on board, and should anyone start to feel thirsty, it's only a pound per bottle. Should you prefer something else to drink, I've also got tea and coffee, which is one pound a cup. If you'd like to come and see me when we stop, I would be more than happy to oblige. Thank you.'

'Blimey, a pound a bottle. That's a bit over the top, ain't it? It's half that price in Sainsbury's,' piped up

Rose.

Rose was right, and it was surely, a signal for an uncomfortable journey ahead.

'Why is the bottled water so expensive?' Mary asked me.

'We're a captive audience,' I replied.

'We don't have to buy the stuff, if we don't want to.'

'Oh yes, you will ... you'll be gasping for a drink,' I said knowingly.

'Why's that, then?'

'Because as soon as we get going the driver will whack the heating up as high as he can, and before long, you'll be begging him for a bottle of water. It'll be hotter than Death Valley,' I replied. 'I wouldn't mind betting the heater is probably the only thing, which works properly on this luxury wreck.'

Chapter 5

We hadn't been travelling for too long when we suddenly came to a grinding halt in the middle of Birmingham; the middle of Erdington, to be more precise. The coach had been slowing down for some time, and I'd noticed the driver was struggling to engage certain gears. There was a smell of burning oil creeping up through the floor of the coach. The driver pulled on the brakes, turned in his seat, and began sorting through the pockets of his jacket. He then stepped out of the coach and onto the grass verge by the side of the road.

'What's he doing? Why have we stopped? Who is he on the phone to?' queried Mary, looking worried.

If I knew the reason why then I'd have been able to supply her with an answer, but I was just as much in the dark as she and the rest of the passengers were. I did have my suspicions, though.

'Ere, Phil ... did you hear that grinding noise?' asked Alan has he leant across. 'I reckon the coach is buggered and he's ringing for help.'

'I did, mate, yes.' I replied. 'I could also smell something funny ... think you might be right ... he's definitely on the phone to someone.'

Mick then tapped me on the shoulder and enquired. 'What's that bloody awful smell, Phil?'

I knew it wasn't my aftershave, because I wasn't wearing any, and besides, Mary had packed it in her suitcase. At that moment our driver climbed back into the coach, and after yet another ear-shattering squeal followed by a God almighty crackling sound, he announced. 'One-two ... one-two ... there has been a technical hitch, but don't worry everyone, help is on its way. In the meantime, I'll put some music on,' and with that, he sorted through a selection of CDs, pushed one of them into the player, and turning round, said, 'Rock on Tommy,' and stepped back off the coach.

This was the closest I have ever come to being involved in a full scale riot. All the passengers looked around at each other, opened mouthed. and for that split second, before the shouting and swearing started, and before threats of lynching were issued, we were as one. According to his choice of music, the wheels on the bus go round and round, round and round, round and round.'

Quickly realising his mistake, the driver dashed straight back onto the coach and thumped the eject button on the CD player, while grabbing the microphone, which, once again, gave out another earwax melting squeal, followed by yet another bloody *one-two, one-two*. 'Sorry folks, I had a coach load of kids on here last week. Here's a song I'm sure you will all enjoy ... something really edgy, and one of my all-time favourites, so take it away, Karen,' the driver said, as he begged for our forgiveness and his life.

No, no, no, no. Edgy? Karen Carpenter, edgy? *We've Only Just Begun* is a lot of things but, edgy, certainly isn't one of them. If she'd still been here today and sitting on this rust bucket, she would most likely have been singing, *We've Barely Just Begun.* That is exactly what had happened; we had barely just begun. We had only been going twenty minutes and here we were stuck on the busy roadside in Erdington.

I am not one for thumb-twiddling - who said patience is a virtue? Well, it's a load of rubbish. I need to be doing something, I do not like sitting around waiting for things to happen. Salvation came in the form of a tatty, rolled up magazine, which a previous passenger, on this apology for private luxury travel, had dropped on the floor. Interesting, I thought, I'll have a quick looksie.

The Warwickshire countryside - a scattering of pretty little towns and villages. There are plenty of charming and pleasant places to visit - castles, old churches, magnificent gardens and stately homes. Spend a day exploring the picturesque countryside. Shop at weekly markets, and treat yourself to a pub lunch from a myriad of wonderful hostelries that are worth a visit. Try a river or a canal trip or take time out for a leisurely walk around Kenilworth Castle or Shakespeare's, Stratford-upon-Avon. But, for Christ's sake ... avoid Erdington.

'What are you reading?' enquired Mary.

'Just a magazine, which I found someone had dropped on the floor.'

'What's it about?'

'It's some sort of visitor's guide, places to visit and see in Warwickshire. Someone's ticked off a few places to have a look at.'

'Does it mention Erdington ... does it tell you where you can get a decent bite to eat? Does it say if there's a Wetherspoons around here somewhere?'

'Erdington? You must be having a laugh,' I replied. 'Erdington should be in a visitor's guide book of places to avoid, I would have thought.'

'Phil's right,' said Mick, looking back over his shoulder. 'It's a right dump.'

'Bloody hell, how long are we going to be stuck here, then?' piped up Rose questioningly.

'We only live just down the road, we could have popped home and had some breakfast,' Chris chipped in.

'Breakfast? Did someone mention breakfast? I'm bloody starving. I could murder a bacon sarnie,' piped up Alan, smacking his lips.

'You're always starving,' said Rose smiling. 'The only time he's not eating, Phil, is when he's sleeping, and even then he's probably dreaming about bacon. He's always waking me up, grunting and grinding his bloody teeth and snuffling into the pillows. Gets on my tits, it does.'

'Ere is that flipping Carpenters CD on a bloody loop or something. If I hear *Ticket to Ride* one more time, I'm going to shove that CD up that driver's....' Chris stopped Mick in mid flow just seconds before he told us where that preferred destination for the CD might be.

Our driver climbed back onto the coach and picked up the microphone, but this time we were all prepared for what followed, and everyone could be seen jamming fingers into their ears.

Lip reading is a technique of understanding what a person is saying, by visually interpreting the movement of their lips, when normal sound is not available. I had a feeling that by the end of the holiday, I would be an expert in this field; that is, if we ever got to start the bloody holiday.

As soon as the driver put the microphone back in its holder, everyone could be seen pulling fingers out of their ears.

'Bloody hell, Alan, look at your fingers. When was the last time you washed your lugholes out? You could grow some spuds in them by the look of it, you could,' said Rose in a loud voice.

'Oiy, you cheeky mare. I wash my ears out every time I wash.'

I immediately picked up on the fact, that he did not qualify his statement, by giving a date or time as to when his last wash was, or when his next wash might be.

'What did the driver say?' queried Alan. 'I couldn't hear a dicky bird.'

'That's because you had your fingers in your ears, you bozo,' replied Rose.

Weren't those Ludwig von Beethoven's last words? *"Sorry I couldn't hear a friggin thing, I'd got my fingers stuck in my lugholes".* In the past, I've often felt the need to stick my fingers in my lugholes when being forced to listen to some of his music. I felt proud of myself, and I reckoned I'd understood most, if not all, of what the driver had said.

'He told those of us, who could lip read, that the long hoped for help would arrive in about an hour and a half,' I informed those around me.

'An hour and a half ... an hour and a bloody half ... we'll never get to Skegness at this bleeding rate,' shouted someone at the back of the coach, who apparently came from Oxford.

I must say, I was shocked to hear an Oxfordian swearing in such a way. How crude, I thought, and with all that education and university types swanning about. Temperatures were rising, women were crying, and Shirley, the woman we'd met at the bus stop in Kenilworth, was bawling her eyes out. Mick, like the knight in shining armour he is, stood up, and diving into his pocket, offered her his handkerchief.

'Here, luv, take this ... it's got a couple of dry corners. What with losing your mum and that, this must be absolute agony for you.'

'It's not losing her mum she's crying about, she's over all that,' said Barry, the poor lady's husband. 'She's sobbing her heart out because she thinks we'll miss tonight's bingo at the hotel.'

'We'll never friggin well get there at this rate,' sobbed Shirley, looking up at Mick. 'I'm having a run of real bad luck at the moment,' she cried as she blew her nose into Mick's handkerchief.

At last, there was movement outside, a police car

had pulled up. Surprise, surprise, it appeared the coppers around here don't say, *"hello, hello, hello, what's all this then?"*. The only words I could hear properly were, *"Get this thing moving or we'll get it moved for you, What's wrong with this wreck?"* and *"Don't ask me, how the hell should I know, I'm not a bleeding mechanic, I'm just the driver ... you'll be having a bloody riot on your hands shortly"*.

Everything seemed to be going terribly wrong. We'd been stuck on the side of a busy road in Birmingham, sorry Erdington, causing traffic chaos, and it looked as if we were going to miss the bingo at the hotel after all. Poor Shirley, she was so looking forward to it.

'They open at nine? What opens at nine?' queried Rose frowning.

'Truckpart,' replied Alan.

'How do you know?'

'I just looked them up on my iPhone.'

'Truckpart, who are they, then?'

'That's where the mechanic is going to have to get the spare part for the coach from.'

'What mechanic?'

'The one who's just turned up, you ninny.'

'We thought you said it would only be an hour and a half?' shouted everyone angrily.

'Sorry folks, twas a slip of the lips,' replied the driver sheepishly. He must have been coughing when he said it.

'I'm going to report him for smoking on the coach, that is, if we ever get back home,' I whispered to Mary.

'Where's the Truckpart place around here, Alan?' enquired Mick.

'I don't know about round here, mate, but according to my iPhone the nearest one is up in Boston.'

'Boston!' exclaimed Rose. 'ere that's in Lincolnshire, ain't it? That's near Skegness ... where we're going. Why can't we pick the spare part thing on the way there?'

As luck would have it there was a spares outlet closer at hand, and when the mechanic had finished fitting it, we were soon up and running once again - by the way it was the fan belt. Everyone was cheering and clapping and some were shouting for an encore, and the coach didn't start moving until the grease monkey - mechanic - had climbed aboard the bus and taken a bow.

One old lady rushed forward and gave him a sloppy kiss, the poor man.

Chapter 6

At last, we were on our way. Panic over, it was time to sit back and enjoy what remained of the journey. There was still plenty of daylight left, and the opportunity to watch the world and the countryside slide by. We crossed the busy Chester Road and headed for Sutton Coldfield, along the A5127 and through Wylde Green. It was a chance to see how the other half lives.

'Ere, Chris ... can you see all those big houses?'

'Yes, Mick,' replied Chris. 'I can see them. I bet not many of the buggers who own them are on PAYE.'

'What's that PAYE thing, then?' Rose queried. 'I've heard of it, but Alan told me not to get involved.'

'It's the system an employer uses to take tax and national insurance from your wages,' I enlightened her.

'Did you know that?' asked Rose, turning to Alan.

'I've heard of it, but I've never been too sure what it all means. Summat about giving money to the government, I think?'

'They explain to you what it's all about when you get your pay packet,' piped up Mick.

'I never saw mine ... it went straight in the bank,'

Alan informed us.

'You never used to look at your pay packet? Why ever not, mate?' I enquired of Alan.

'I did once, Phil, but it looked all complicated to me. Blimey, it was years ago, when I was working as a trainee tea maker.'

'Toolmaker? I never knew you were a toolmaker.'

'I wasn't, Mick ... I said tea maker. It was the first job I had after I left school. A three year apprenticeship, so it was. I know all the recipes, and when I finished that, I went off to Cambridge University.'

'Blimey ... Cambridge University. How long did you go there for, then?'

'I went nearly every day for three years. Jesus, it was a balls ache, all that bloody driving. They were long days, they were, starting out at four in the morning to get there and back by ten o'clock at night, five days a week.'

'D'you know, mate ... I might have misjudged you. I hadn't realised that you studied at Cambridge University. Which course were you on, then?' I asked rather curious.

''Ere Alan, you ain't got one of them HPDs, have you? You ain't a master of summat or other?' queried Chris.

'Master ... HPDs ... what in the hell are you on about, and what has me going to Cambridge University got to do with courses?' retorted Alan huffily.

'You just told us you spent three years going to

Cambridge University,' I replied.

'I did, every day. I used to deliver loads of teabags and stuff to the student's refectories at the various colleges, and then carry on into the city centre and do a few drop-offs there. Courses ... what courses ... I never went on any courses apart from my teamaking one. Sorry, that's a lie, I did go on one once.'

'Where was that?' questioned Mick with curiosity.

'I went to Warwick Racecourse once, mate. Sorry, I'd forgotten that,' replied Alan looking serious.

Chris was right after all. Alan wasn't a master of anything, apart from that of self abuse.

As we drove towards the town centre in Sutton Coldfield, we passed a favourite watering hole of Mick, Alan and myself, *The Bottle Of Sack*, a Tim Martin magnificence on the Birmingham Road.

'We've had a few good times in there, haven't we lads,' laughed Mick.

Oh dear, Mick should have kept his mouth shut. Chris immediately folded her arms across her chest, after first pulling the edges of her cardigan together. She adjusted her bra straps, while giving him the pigeon nod. I noticed a lump suddenly appeared in Mick's throat, followed by an audible gulping sound.

'So you've had some good times in there, have you, Michael?'

You can tell when a woman gets angry, she calls her husband by his birth name, and not by the shortened or affectionate form of it.

'Would you like to tell me, Mary and Rose all about these *good* times, then? I'm sure they're as interested as I am to hear what you lot have been getting up to when you're out on the town without us supervising and holding your hands,' questioned Chris emphatically. 'I think us girls need to hear this, don't we?'

There is a God after all. Mick's grovelling words were cut short when a wired, unidirectional dynamic microphone, screamed into action with an excruciating squeal and another *"one-two, one-two"*.

'Bloody hell, what was that?' shouted Barry, the husband of sobbing Shirley who, incidentally, was no longer sobbing, but appeared to be fondling two bingo card dabbers. Presumably, she'd brought two because she was afraid she might run out, and I noticed they were both red. Perhaps her lucky colour.

'Ladies and gents,' barked our driver. 'Shortly we will be making a required stop as I have just noticed on my tachograph that I need to take a short break. Don't blame me, it's those idiot sprouts in Brussels that make all the rules. It won't be long, about an hour should do it, and I will find a suitable place to pull over. Although we do have a toilet on the coach, I would ask all of you to restrict its use to that of number ones only, please ... no big jobs, thank you,' and with a here we are, the driver moved the coach over to the left and pulled up next to a gateway on the Sutton Road close by the local crematorium.

'Did he say no big jobs? I'm desperate, I am,' whispered one of the men to his wife.

Poor bloke, I thought, pretending I hadn't heard. I'd wondered why his forehead was running with sweat.

'Ere, driver,' shouted the man's wife. 'My husband is touching cloth, so what's he supposed to do?'

There was a hushed silence, and everyone near the front looked back to see who had asked the driver this most embarrassing question, craning their heads to see whose face was the reddest and who was sweating the most.

'We will be making a toilet stop at Tamworth. For all those touching cloth, like the gentleman at the back, if you can't hold it in, you'll just have to get off the coach and use the hedge,' the driver shouted back.

'It'll have to do,' her husband said turning to his wife. 'I'm desperate, and I only brought along one pair of trousers.'

We must have been sitting there for at least half an hour when Mick leant across and asked, the by now much-relieved husband, who had only an hour before, an embarrassing problem, if the hedgerow afforded enough privacy. Interested as to what the chap's reply was Chris turned to Mick and asked what he'd said.

'He told me to watch where I was stepping, if I was going to off-load,' whispered Mick. 'We are obviously not the only ones who've stopped here.'

Our coach had stopped near the southern border with Staffordshire, and a short distance from a bridge, which crossed the busy M6 toll road. There was little to see through the windows, because although we were sitting pretty high up, the hedges alongside this busy road were much higher.

We were all bored. A few of the passengers had

taken to litter spotting, and I heard one lady saying, *"I spy with my little eye something beginning with D"*. I never did find out what the D represented because the obvious answer *Driver* was immediately ruled out.

God, it was so irritating, there was the driver sitting on the grass verge beside the coach, and with the bottom few inches of his trousers rolled up, puffing on a fag. Now and again he pushed a finger up his nose or dug something out of one of his ears. At the same time, he was talking to someone on his iPhone, seemingly oblivious to the constant blasting of car horns from drivers, who were adjudging the position of the coach at the side of this busy road, as extremely dangerous. It was only after he'd given a V sign to the irritated driver of a flatbed truck, who'd shouted *Wanker* to him and then slowed his vehicle down, intending to stop, that our driver quickly got to his feet and jumped back onto the coach. His bravado had suddenly deserted him and fear had obviously kicked in.

It was once again time to press our fingers into our ears, and after the annoying, and totally unnecessary, *"one-two, one-two"* the driver informed us it was now time to get going. 'Right ladies and gents, we are back on the road and our next stop will be Tamworth, where our last pick up will be and you will have the opportunity to go to the toilet and grab a bit of lunch.'

We had been looking forward to this. We'd been on the road since eight o'clock that morning, and it was now twelve noon and we'd barely travelled twenty five miles. A journey that should have taken approximately forty minutes had taken five bloody hours.

A romance of the countryside needs no preamble. If the first impression one gets of this part of our landlocked country is uniformity, the second must be of its surprises and hidden secrets. Tamworth is one of those secrets. Up until now, we had not had any form of commentary from our driver; no snippets of interesting information. To be fair, it had only been five hours since we started out on, what was for us an epic journey, but the passengers who were already on the coach, which had started its journey in Southampton, had already been told about our part of the world. Were we now to hear some mind boggling secrets about someone else's, I wonder.

'So, is this where they make the snuff and mint cake?' I heard someone asking.

A lady, who was sitting in a seat in front of mine and Mary's, turned round and said. 'Well, I'll go to the foot of our stairs. Our driver is a mine of information, you know. So knowledgeable he is ... isn't he Reg?'

'Yes, he is ... I don't know where he gets all his information from,' replied Reg, who was sitting beside her. 'I never knew they dance around in skirts, and blow the bagpipes in Reading. They were invented in Winchester, you know.'

'What was?' I asked him.

'The devices used to hold pieces of paper together ... paper clips,' he replied.

How fascinating is that, I thought to myself. You learn something new every day, and if there is a book on paper clips then surely I must have it. I wondered whether or not our driver was married and if he was, who the lucky lady must be and what a lucky lady she must be, to be married to someone who knows so much about mint cake, bagpipes and paper clips.

'The driver is a founder member of the Paper Clip Collectors Club, you know,' Reg informed us.

Our coach pulled across the entrance to Morrisons car park in Offa Drive, where the last passengers were to be picked up. People, who had finished their shopping, were trapped in their cars, and prevented from exiting the car park, and likewise those who had hoped to gain access were prevented from doing so until our driver had loaded the two cases onto the coach and finished smoking the cigarette he'd decided to light up. He appeared totally oblivious to the cacophony of car horns, and shouts of *"Get out the bleeding way, you tosser"* and *"Wanker"* from irate motorists. He was none too pleased when he finally climbed back up behind the steering wheel.

'I don't know why these people think it's a joke to sound off like that. All that noise was doing my head in. They're all out on a jolly, while I'm working. I've got my job to do,' he moaned loudly.

And while he was on the subject of doing people's heads in, he decided it was time to get his own back on humanity, by testing out his microphone once again.

'Right, ladies and gents ... that was our last pick up, Mr and Mrs Walley. From here on it should be plain sailing, our next stop, Skegness, so sit back and enjoy the views. I'll put some nice music on to help you all relax.

'About friggin time,' shouted one of the passengers.

'I hope he puts something decent on,' piped up Mick.

'A bit of ELO would be nice,' said Chris.

'What, like *Mister Blue Sky*?'

'Yes, Rose,' replied Chris. 'That's Mick's favourite song, ain't it?'

'Yes, Chris ... it is love.'

Sadly, Mick was out of luck.

'You're all going to enjoy this one, ladies and gents ... *The Girl With The Giggle*,' shouted our driver.

'Who the hell is *The Girl With The Giggle*?' queried Rose, looking rather bemused.

'You're too young to remember,' I replied.

'Yes, who is it, Phil, remind me?' asked Mary.

'Alma Cogan.'

'Who the hell is Alma bloody Cogan?' queried Alan, frowning.

Thank goodness I'd had the presence of mind to bring two handkerchiefs so I could block both my ears.

Chapter 7

I cannot remember how long I had been asleep. The last thing I did remember, it was still daylight and the driver was telling us all about the time, when some bloke called Barry Lineker played for the Leicester Tigers. Apparently, it was a darts or cricket team, or maybe something else. Whatever he was telling us about had sent me to sleep; it was that interesting.

I had missed Nottingham, Newark and Lincoln. I had hoped to catch a glimpse of Horncastle, where my father had stayed during World War Two, but I was in the land of nod at the time. Besides, I wouldn't have been able to see anything as it was pitch black.

It seemed I had been asleep for quite a while, and I suddenly found myself wide awake, an unusual experience for me. I knew the disturbance had come, not from outside of me, but from within, from some low but persistent knock on the remote door of consciousness. Most dreams are purely trivial and a sign of a weak and derisory nature, to pay attention to them. Only occasionally do they matter, and this one mattered. She was blonde and beautiful, had bits in the right place, and where they mattered most, and that is all I could recall. Suddenly, I was awake again.

'Ere, what's going on, it's dark now. Where in the hell are we ... have we arrived?' I asked. 'Is this Skegness?'

'No, we bloody well haven't, and I haven't a clue where we are,' replied Mary grumpily.

'This is getting beyond a joke,' exclaimed Mick. 'Where's the bloody driver gone? Wake up Chris, you've been annoying everyone with your snoring. You sound like a flippin lawnmower.'

'Sorry luv, it's my teeth. I have to sleep with my mouth closed, to stop my lips flapping and my teeth falling out.'

'Alan, are you and Rose awake?' I quietly asked. 'Have you any idea where we are? Have they put the clocks back or something ... we are still in British summertime, ain't we?'

'Mick's wrong, Phil,' replied Alan angrily. 'It's way beyond a bloody joke. I've just seen the driver get off and head back to a pub we've just passed. He's been gone a bloody long time, he has. If he comes back pissed there'll be merry hell to play.'

As if by magic, our driver suddenly reappeared. 'Sorry folks, I've found out where I'm going now.'

I looked at Mary and she looked at Rose, who was looking at Alan and he was looking at Mick, who was looking at Chris. We were looking at one another with incredulity.

'Found out where you're going? What do you mean you've found out where you're going? You're meant to be taking us to Skegness. Have you never been there before, then? What the hell do you mean,

"I've found out where I'm going"?' shouted someone from the rear.

It was at this point the microphone and its crippling sound once again burst upon our increasingly fragile eardrums.

'One-two, one-two. Ladies and gents, I'm sorry about that but I got a little lost back there, and had to pop to the pub and make a phone call,' our driver announced.

That's funny, I thought. He had been speaking on a mobile earlier, so why would he need to go back to a pub to make a telephone call?

'There's a page missing from the atlas they gave me, so I decided to turn the Satnav on, but the company has just had it fitted and it looks as though the idiot who fitted it, hasn't set the bloody thing up correctly; looks as if it's made in Germany. When I switched it on it kept saying something like *"Beiden Sie sofort links ab"* and *"Poland this way"*. Where the hell's Poland ... is it near Skegness? Does anyone know?' enquired our driver. 'Anyway, we should be at the hotel by three o'clock, it's only about five miles down the road. I have telephoned ahead to the friendly hotel ambassador, whose name is Kevin Hiscock, and he has informed me that he will stay awake for us and on arrival will direct each one of you to your rooms. By the way, the hotel lift is out of action and apologies in advance for the inconvenience, but someone has buggered about with it and, as a result, the main electrics have tripped off. Don't worry, he said, for a small extra charge you can pick up a candle at reception. All those who do not smoke can come to me and I'll be only too happy to provide a light ... at no extra charge, although you might like to see me in the bar tomorrow night ... if you get my drift. Thank you.'

'You've been asleep for hours, you have. We've had two toilet stops while you've been snoring away. I reckon we killed all the grass in that last layby,' said Mary.

'Can I claim on our medical insurance, Jim?' a woman asked her husband.

'Why's that, Babs. Ere you ain't hurt yourself, have you luv?'

'Yes, I think I might have, Jim.'

'Oh, dear. What's happened, sweetheart?'

'Squatting down on some brambles was bad enough, but there was a load of stingers in amongst them. I'll have to sleep on my front,' replied Babs.

'I've stung and scratched my arse as well,' piped up another woman.

'I reckon I should charge the bus company for cleaning the side of the coach,' said Bab's husband, Jim.

Everyone was becoming more than a little irritated. Misphrased and ill-timed comments were leading to full scale arguments. Reminders of long-ago mistakes were suddenly dragged into the present.

'You know I don't like dogs,' another woman was heard to say.

'Dogs? What are you on about dogs for? We haven't got a dog ... Nobby died years ago. In fact we haven't had a dog for over forty years,' her husband replied.

'Yes, I know, but I haven't forgotten. Nobby bit a hole in my hot pants.'

'That's because he got excited when you walked into the room wearing them. You took him by surprise. Oiy, and what about the time you burned that bloody great hole in my trousers, then?'

'It wasn't my fault ... it was yours,' she replied indignantly.

'Mine ... how d'ya work that one out?'

'You made me do it. Forcing me to iron your clothes. You'll be getting me to wash and iron my own next, you beast.'

Poor Nobby, poor bloke. What other mistakes had he made in the past forty years of their marriage? There was still time for us to find out.

We eventually came to a halt. I could hear the howling of a dog, and see the flickering of a torch. At long last we had arrived, and our driver was right, someone really had made a dog's dinner of the hotel lift, there wasn't one light on anywhere. The only glimmer I could see was a tiny one moving from side to side.

'Jesus, what have I put my foot in,' exclaimed the driver, as he stepped from the coach. 'Oh, for God's sake. Bloody hell what a mess ... Jesus it stinks.'

Holding the other end of a flickering torch was the skinny shape of someone in an ill-fitting uniform and a malfunctioning peaked cap, which he was desperately trying to stop from falling over the front of his eyes and face. He appeared to have some difficulty climbing onto the coach. Could he also be wearing a pair of thirty-two inch inside leg trousers, which were flopping against a set of twenty-nine inch inside legs, similar to me in my pyjamas? If this was the case, then I certainly knew how he was feeling.

He was as taken aback as we all were, when he grabbed hold of the microphone and woke everybody up on the whole of the East Coast of England. After his initial shock, his cap flopped back down and rested on the top edge of a pair of sellotaped glasses that he was wearing.

'Hello everybody, welcome to sunny Skegness. My name is Kevin Hiscock, but please no names ... no pack drill ... you can call me Kevin.'

Kevin? A woman carried him for thirty-six weeks, went through hours of painful labour and contractions and after he appeared on the scene, named him Kevin? Was it really worth all that effort? I was beginning to get rather concerned.

'I am here to ensure that you have a great time,' continued Kevin. 'Breakfast is served between five and six each morning, and tomorrow's offering is cornflakes, sausage on toast, egg on toast, or bacon on toast. Oh, yes, and a glass of orange juice. I'm sorry you missed the bingo but tomorrow night there will be a disco in Kev's Cave ... that's me by the way. I will be playing plenty of popular hits from the likes of The Carpenters, The Bachelors, The Funboy Three, and lots more. Are there any ... oh, bloody hell ... what the....'

Oh dear, Mr Kevin Hiscock had suddenly

disappeared, and without warning. One minute he was talking to us all and the next he was gone.

'Bloody hell, where's he gone ... he's disappeared,' I heard someone asking.

'He's fallen off the friggin coach, that's what's happened,' replied someone at the front.

'Oh my God, is he dead?' asked someone else with concern.

It was pitch black when we finally got off the coach. Someone had told us the hotel was only a couple of minutes walk from Skegness's fine sandy beach; just across the road. I knew it was late, but I still expected to see a lot of people, particularly the younger ones, walking around. It was all strangely silent.

'Careful everyone, please be careful where you're stepping, and watch out for the dog. Don't go near him,' our driver informed us. 'Kevin has lost the battery in his torch, so you could go arse over tit, like him, if you don't watch your step. Remember, watch out for his dog, Masher.'

I looked out the coach window and could see this Kevin idiot fiddling with his empty torch, and when he eventually found it, managing to re-install the battery.

'Found it ... I've found it, and it's working again,' Kevin could be heard shouting triumphantly, while at the same time laughing in embarrassment. 'I've found the battery ... normal service has been restored. Oh no, bloody hell.' Our meeter and greeter, our concierge, was suddenly cut short.

'What's up, mate. Is it bust?' queried our driver.

'The battery's rolled in summat really nasty ... can't you smell it?' replied Kevin screwing up his nose.

'Phew, you're right. Jesus, it bloody stinks.'

'Walk this way everyone, please,' shouted Kevin. 'Take care on the step and when we get to reception, I'll give you all the key to your rooms.'

'Step, did he say?' queried Chris. 'There's at least twenty of them. It's like walking up a bloody mountainside. You be careful Mick ... here take my handbag, will you please?'

As if he wasn't struggling enough, Mick now had to carry his wife's crown jewels.

'Handbag!' exclaimed Mick. 'I'm tugging two flippin great cases, woman. What am I supposed to do with your handbag?'

'Hang it round your neck, you silly bugger. Where do you think? Us girls don't half pick em,' she said, raising her eyebrows and looking back at Mary and Rose. 'I can't manage the room key and a candle, now can I?'

Mick and Chris had found it difficult to identify their cases in the dark, and they were not the only ones. Everyone had the same problem, and then having to haul them up Skegness's equivalent of Mount Kilimanjaro.

'Ere are you trying to nick my suitcase?' someone asked.

'If you bust my hair straightener, you're dead,' shouted someone else.

I had a vision of a funeral director turning up in the morning to take a body, or even several bodies, away.

'Phil, is there any chance you giving Alan a hand with our cases, please?' asked Rose sweetly. 'He's just told me he's feeling dizzy. Apparently, the steps are too steep for him, he thinks he might have altitude sickness, or something. He gets giddy and has a nose bleed if he even thinks about climbing a ladder. When we had that window cleaning round, it was me who went up the ladder, while he stood at the bottom wringing out the shammy. I told him not to wear those thick socks of his, the silly sod.'

I resisted the temptation of giving the poor old sod an applause, but somehow I thought it wouldn't go down too well.

'Okay, no problem,' I replied. 'Tell him to stop where he is and I'll come back just as soon as I've got mine and Mary's case into the reception.'

'Oh, you are kind, Phil. Thanks a lot.'

At long last, we had finally made it. What a relief from what had been an ordeal for all of us. It had taken nineteen hours to get to the Hotel Lost Vagas Extra on the Middlemarsh Road in Skegness. Some of our fellow passengers, poor buggers, had been on the coach for almost twenty-four hours. The coach's German Satnav could have got us to Berlin in the same time it had taken to get from Kenilworth to Skegness.

It was difficult to see at first but a sign on the wall behind reception suggested calm and reassurance - *"More dreams are realised in our hotel, than in any other hotel in England. Our hospitality makes our guests feel as though they are staying in the comfort of their own homes".* It was made more poignant by the gentle flickering of candlelight. This was just what we had hoped for, a home from home. A lovely relaxing holiday in one of the best, if not the best, hotels in England.

'Here we are Mr and Mrs Sleet ... room 48. Ah yes, it's one of our themed rooms ... *Love's Sweet Dream*. A good room that one, everything works, except for the door, the local coppers kicked it down during a drugs bust; it seems that the last occupiers were doing a bit of dealing, so I was told. We have to replace the lock, and at present, we have had to make use of a padlock until the maintenance manager can source a replacement. It shouldn't be too much of a problem ... *Love's Sweet Dream* is at the rear. The stairs are over there behind you and don't forget to take a candle, you might need it. Yesterday, one of our guests tripped on a loose part of the carpet, and the silly berk went head over heels and bust his leg. His antics gave me and the missus a right laugh. It was like watching Charlie Cairoli and Billy Smart's circus all over again. Mrs Hiscock reckons he was pissed. *"Have you ever seen an eighty-year-old do a stupid thing like that,"* she said. Anyway, that'll be our defence in court. He obviously hadn't read the *Take Care On The Stair* notice, stupid old bastard. There's absolutely no way we're going to pay for his new hip.'

Everything sounded so beautiful. A scene, which can only be seen in this beautiful country of ours. A scene that challenges both the poet and the painter.

Windows framed in a low-browed ceiling of a hotel, which sits on the edge of a meadow, overlooking a sandy beach and sparkling blue sea. The general silence broken, only by the sound of running water over a pebble beach and birds fluttering past an open window. *Love's Sweet Dream* - what a load of stuff and nonsense it turned out to be, although it could have been a lot worse. Alan and Rose had been given *Room for Romance,* and even worse still, Mick and Chris were stopping in *Dungangbangin*. Mary and I were eager to hear what that was all about.

'I hope they get that lift sorted soon,' said Mary. 'It's going to be a struggle for you, climbing up and down these stairs each morning and evening, with my handbag.'

I also hoped it would be. Hauling a heavy suitcase, a holdall, along with a handbag, full of God knows what, wrapped round my neck was anything but a joke.

'I forgot to tell that Kevin bloke we're vegetarians,' I said, turning to Mary.

I had no idea why I'd suddenly decided to take ownership of that statement. If Mary received a banger on a plate for her breakfast, then my life would not be worth living. Yet another example of an uncaring husband, perhaps?

After nearly ten minutes struggling with the padlock, I decided I would need to contact reception and ask for help.

'Come here,' Mary said sounding rather grumpy and fed up. 'I can't hang about for that bozo. Get out of the bloody way.'

With the help of a not insubstantial shoulder barge and a size six boot, we finally managed to break into our room, and with further help from the candle, which true to his word, our driver had lit, I managed to see a pair of twin beds in the dim flickering light.

'I brought a bag with me,' I said to Mary. 'I'm going to nick all the little bottles of shampoo and bars of soap. We've paid a lot of money for this holiday.'

I made it to the nearest bed and dropped onto it. I was exhausted, but suddenly there was a splintering cracking sound.

'Sod it, I have just gone and broken a leg.'

'You haven't?' queried my sympathetic wife. 'Well that's sure as hell buggered my holiday up, hasn't it? What a selfish sod you are ... why couldn't you have waited until we got back home?'

'No, you daft fool. I haven't broken my leg ... I've broken one of the legs off the bloody bed. That's what I've broken.'

'What leg? The bed hasn't got any legs ... it's standing on piles of books. You ain't done no damage, you've just ruined a copy of William Makepeace Thackeray's *Vanity Fair*. I'm sure they must have another book around here somewhere. Ah, here we are, *Right Bed Wrong Guy* ... try this,' and she handed me the book.

'I've never heard of the author Betty Swallocks before. Have you, Phil?'

Surprisingly enough, I hadn't as it happened.

Chapter 8

At first, I failed. I found it was nigh on impossible to roll over. Apart from it being the most uncomfortable of beds to sleep on, I can honestly say, I have never slept on a mattress full of house bricks before but, in my imagination, this is exactly what it felt like, and it was the most difficult of beds to get out of.

Were Mary and I the victims of some practical joke? When I first saw the bed, I did think it looked slightly suspicious, balanced as it was on three short legs and a William Makepiece Thackery literary masterpiece. The moment I stretched out I found myself sinking to the floor on the mattress. When I looked up I could just about make out Mary, who appeared to be sleeping two floors above me, in the next bed.

Once again I tried, and once again I failed miserably. It felt as if I was sticking to something. Grabbing the side of the wooden bed frame, I gingerly and very slowly pulled it towards me, and whatever I'd been holding came apart and gave way. I rolled off the mattress and onto the carpet, and when I did eventually manage to stand up, discovered the bedsheets were hanging from me.

A housekeeper, or assistant, must visit each room twice a day. In the morning they should pick up a plan of the hotel rooms and inspect each room to check which have been occupied, and if the bed has been used, and if there is luggage, they should check that too, and then report to the reception by 9 o'clock. In the afternoon, when the rooms have been cleaned, whoever is in charge, should carefully examine each room, and if there is a torn sheet or pillowcase, then they should make a note of it. There may be a shortage of towels and soap in some rooms, so this should also be noted. In corners, she may find *Irish curtains* - spiders webs - or a forgotten cup or glass. Some cleaners may have swept the centre of the room, while dust, which has lain for two weeks or more, remains under the bed and cupboards. In another room, they might find the bath or shower has completely been forgotten.

'Wake up Phil,' I heard Mary shouting. 'We'll be late for breakfast, and if Alan and Rose get down there first there'll be bugger all left. You know what they're like ... a pair of bloody gannets.'

Wake up. I hadn't had a sleep to wake up from.

'I'm tired,' I said sleepily. 'What time is breakfast?'

'That Kevin bloke said it was starting at five o'clock,' Mary replied.

'What time is it now, then?'

'Ten to.'

'Ten to? Why the hell didn't you wake me earlier? For God's sake, how long in hell have I been asleep for?'

'Nearly two hours.'

'Two hours ... two bloody hours ... is that all? That's hardly enough time to get my jim-jams on.'

'You haven't got them on, you're still wearing what you had on when we arrived at stupid o'clock this morning. You dropped onto the bed, knocked the bed leg off its book support, and fell fast asleep. I've only just managed to get my make-up off, and I haven't even unpacked yet.'

'Right-i-o,' I said jumping up. 'We'd better get a move on.'

'Yes, and don't forget to tell Kevin that we're vegetarians. I don't want any ears, eyes or bloody arseholes on my fried bread, thank you very much. And while you're at it tell him there's no shampoo or soap in our room, just dust and Irish curtains everywhere, and the shower doesn't work. Oh, and ask him where the hell the bath is? I can't find one anywhere.'

Standing up a little to quickly, and with a rush of blood to my head, I walked to the bedroom door. I hadn't noticed when we'd entered our room a couple of hours as I was that tired.

'What's this then?' I queried. 'The bloody door's half-open. It's that padlock ... we could have been murdered in our beds.'

It was the police's fault, the ones who kicked the door down. I know it's part of their training, but come on, let's get real, why don't they just knock first? Bloody vandals.

'What else is wrong in this dump?'

'The toilet,' replied Mary.

'And what's wrong with that, dare I ask?'

'There's no seat.'

'It flushes, I hope?'

'In a fashion.'

'How do you mean, in a fashion?'

'You have to tug a chain above which, by the way, we haven't got.'

'Chain? The toilet has a chain? You have to be joking? I thought they went out with the Ark.'

Did Noah's Ark have a toilet chain? Did it even have a toilet? Were there two of them, like there were two of each of the animals? Or did he and his wife, Naamah, and their sons Shem, Ham and Japheth just fill a bucket and chuck it?

'I'm sure if we ask, Kevin will come and fix it for us,' I said to Mary.

'Yes, and while you're there, don't forget to ask him if we can have a chain, will you?'

We stumbled out our room, and I decided not to spend time trying to fit the padlock as we didn't want to risk missing breakfast and starving to death. After all, clothes are no good to anyone who's died of starvation.

Progress down the stairs was perilous; Kevin had made us aware of a possible trip hazard, but he'd used the word *trip* in the singular tense and not the plural. There were four flights of them and every step was a trip hazard. When we finally reached the bottom, the man himself was there waiting, wringing his hands and grinning obsequiously, ready to direct us into the restaurant.

'Good morning Mr and Mrs Sleet,' he greeted us, lowering his head as he did so.

When I pointed out all the problems that we had found with our room, and the poor state of the stair carpet, he told me that he was aware of a few problems, but thanked me for bringing them to his attention and informed me that everything would be rectified at the earliest opportunity. This included the stair carpet, which was being replaced within the next few days.

I use the term, restaurant, loosely because, in reality, it was nothing more than a large carpetless room with camping tables at the one end and a row of picnic tables and chairs at the other. Alan and Rose were standing by the tables at the head of the queue, each holding a plate. Typical of them, I thought. I signalled to him and asked where he'd got their plates from.

'Behind you, mate,' he replied, and sure enough that was exactly where they were.

I thought it best to grab a couple and walked back to get them, but when I tried to rejoin the queue, others, who'd since joined the end started to get rather irate. Shirley, the lady we had spoken to on the coach, the one sobbing her heart out over the loss of her mother, told me to *sod off*, and get to the back of the queue. Barry, her husband, was equally belligerent, threatening to set his wife onto me if I tried to push in, and didn't do what Shirley demanded.

I had left the queue when I was only six people

from the front, but now, all of a sudden, I found I was at the very end. Worse still, the plates I had picked up had somehow missed out on the cleaning process. They were dirty and greasy and I had a vision of Kevin's dog, Masher, licking each plate, while Mrs H wiped them dry.

Mary came looking for me then, and got quite angry when I told her what had happened. I had to use all my powers of diplomacy and persuasion to stop her from punching Shirley's lights out.

'I knew she was trouble when I saw her blabbing at the bus stop in Kenilworth,' shouted Mary. 'I've told Kevin we're both vegetarians, and he said for us to go and sit down and he will bring our breakfast across to us. Told me he didn't get too many vegetarians in the hotel, so it would be a good test of the chef's culinary skills. He wanted to know if we liked margarine, but I told him no, we would prefer butter.'

As we walked past the erstwhile Shirley in the queue, whom I'd had issues with only a moment or two before, I smiled wryly and whispered, 'Waitress service,' to which she scowled and signalled to Barry to deck me.

We sat and waited for what seemed an age. Suddenly I saw Kevin, and he was grinning like a Cheshire cat as he walked towards us with two plates expertly balanced on his outstretched arms.

'Here we are then Mr and Mrs Sleet, your vegetarian breakfasts,' and with a flourish he placed a plate in front of each of us.

'What's this?' I queried.

'It's the vegetarian breakfast you ordered, sir.'

'Yeah, but what is it ... vegetarian what?'

'Bread,' replied Kevin, still grinning.

'Bread? A single slice of bread,' said Mary in astonishment.

'Yes, madam, you're very observant. A single slice of bread.'

'Where's the butter?' I enquired.

'We don't have butter, we only use margarine as it's cheaper, but you told me you didn't want margarine. I can get you both a knob of butter, but that will incur an extra charge.'

'What about jam ... is there no jam to go with it?'

'Sorry sir, but the holiday company you booked through doesn't pay us enough to provide jam.'

'So that's it then. A single slice of bread, it's a bloody good job we're not vegans.'

'I can take it back and toast it, if you'd like.'

Mary and I had had enough of this. We left our table and made for the exit of the so-called dining room, and on our way out, we stopped to speak to Alan and Rose, to see what their thoughts were on the breakfast offering.

The *not much* comment was predictable, and it transpired that Alan had been first in the breakfast queue, because when he stepped off the coach at three o'clock in the morning, he had headed straight for the dining room and waited there until Rose joined him.

'I was going to make sure I got a sausage. Bacon and egg would have been nice but Kevin told us it was either-or. What sort of a dump is this place?' Alan asked me, shrugging his shoulders.

After our joke of a breakfast, Mary and I decided to get a bit of fresh air, so we stepped outside to see what we had been unable to on first arriving at the hotel in complete darkness. The sky was blue and the air fresh, and it was time to breathe in the benefits of a sea breeze and soak up the life-giving energy of the sun. Kevin had previously said that the sun was warmer, the sky bluer and the sea the calmest it had been for quite a while. He also told us to steer clear of Masher, his loving little monster, saying - *"I let him roam around the gardens, he keeps the Sheriffs away. Always after money they are."*.

It made for grim viewing. The word *hotel* certainly turned out to be more than a contradiction in terms, and one that could possibly be challenged under the Trades Description Act.

I had expected to see a grand old house, with large lawns, drenched in the quiet first light of a summer morning. To experience a perfect stillness and comfort, which irresistibly appeals to a heart that longs for rest and relaxation. I had also hoped to hear the sound of water flowing through from a pebble beach.

At first I could not decide whether the old building I was looking at, had at some point in the past been something else. It looked like an abandoned factory, which had been turned into a building of multiple occupation, appearing more like a hostel for the economically and socially disadvantaged.

Where were the grandiose architectural details, the

gargantuan domed ceilings and the sweeping staircase? Where had the columns and highly decorated walls and facades gone? People could blame the weather and its effects for being the fundamental reason for all the decay we were now staring at, but that all appeared contrived. The lack of maintenance, the blocked gutters and the damp walls, the ill-considered and inappropriate alterations with the inclusion of steel bars on the windows. How could I have been so stupid, as to mistake the sound of wrecked vehicles being crushed in a breaker's yard directly opposite, to that of the sea rushing onto a pebble strewn beach?

They say that a weed is just a flower growing in the wrong place. Whoever said that, was wrong. The weeds, and there were plenty of them, definitely enhanced what could be better described as a slum.

'What a dump,' said Mary, looking around. 'Let's go back inside.'

I had also seen enough, so we wandered back up to our room, negotiating the distressed and dangerous stair carpet on the way. I was knackered already and we had only just arrived. I now fully understood the adage, the philosophical aphorism that communicates an important truth drawn from experience, about having to take a holiday to get over a holiday, and it was only the start of the second day.

Fortunately, our room was exactly as we had left it. I drew back the curtain - oh yes, it was only a single curtain - to take in the view of the sea and beach.

'Where's it gone?' queried Mary. 'Is the tide out,

do you think?'

'I have no idea,' I replied bemused. 'I know we're at the back of the hotel but I did think we might just be able to see a smidgeon of it, if the window was open and we leant out as far as we safely could. We'll have to walk back down to reception and have a look from the front of the hotel.'

We headed back downstairs, holding on for grim death, to anything that felt safe enough to grasp.

'Where's the sea, Kevin? You told us it was only a few minutes away from the hotel. Is the tide out, or has it gone on strike?' I jokingly enquired, raising my eyebrows.

'It is. Would you like me to order a taxi?'

'It is *what*, Kevin?' I queried.

'The sea ... it's only a few minutes away,' he replied, flashing a quick smile.

'Yes, I heard what you said,' I replied. 'But how do we get there?'

' I can order you a taxi,' repeated Kevin.

'A taxi ... a flippin taxi ... a taxi to the beach. Where the hell is it, for God's sake?'

'Just a short way, Mr Sleet.'

'Look mate. Ordering a taxi to go to the beach suggests to me, that it's not just a few minutes walk away,' I replied somewhat angrily.

'Your holiday company should have told you.'

'How far is it, then?'

'Not far.'

'How far is not far?' I asked once more.

'It's fairly flat ... there are no hills.'

'For God's sake, how far is the Loss bloody Vagas Hotel Extra from the friggin beach?'

'Just over three miles.'

'And what, might I dare to ask, does just over three miles mean?'

'Four and a bit.'

'Four and a bit? What do you mean, four and a bit? Spit it out, mate.'

'It's five actually,' Kevin replied sheepishly. 'We have some binoculars behind reception if you'd like a closer look. They're very good ones, quite strong. I got them off eBay ... an absolute bargain, they were.'

I was not happy man. 'Can you get us a taxi in about an hour ... please?'

Once again we dragged ourselves back up the four flights of stairs to our room. I wanted to change as I was still in the clothes I'd had on for the past twenty-four hours, and I desperately needed a wash and shave.

'Can you give reception a ring, Mary, and ask them for Alan and Rose's room number, and Mick and Chris's as well, while I get ready, please.'

'I would if I could,' came the reply, 'but the telephone, like everything else in this dump, doesn't appear to be connected. I think it's just for show and there's no cable to plug in.'

As luck would have it, Alan, Rose, Mick and Chris were looking through a few brochures at the reception desk when we found our way back down, yet again, after cleaning ourselves up.

'We're going into Skegness,' I announced. 'Would

you all like to accompany us and share the taxi I've asked Kevin to order?'

Looking at one another, they all nodded in agreement.

'That sounds like a very good idea, Phil. We can share the fare,' Mick answered for everyone.

After about five minutes, Kevin, our friendly porter appeared at our side. 'Your taxi is ready and waiting Mr Sleet.'

We followed him to the front of the hotel and down the steps to a battered old car, which was waiting with its engine idling and struggling to keep ticking over.

'Right, where do you want me to drop you off?'

'Where is the taxi driver?' I asked, looking rather dubious.

'I am the taxi driver,' replied Kevin, rather haughtily. 'We provide a full service here, you know ... competitive rates and all that. Are you all going? If so, the fare will be thirty pounds.'

Competitive rates? I wanted to hire a taxi, not buy one. I was brought up properly by my parents and therefore, too refined to describe the unrealistic price, other than to say, it was unambitious. Oh sod it, I'll say it. It was daylight, bloody robbery.

The rather bumpy journey into Skegness gave us a little time to compare notes. Mary and I, as it turned out, were not the only ones who had issues. Alan and Rose had promised to lend Mick and Chris the chain from their toilet, in exchange for a few sheets of toilet paper, plus Chris's pork sausage on the following morning's breakfast extravaganza.

'You're welcome to that, mate,' said Chris. 'Heaven knows what it was made from? There was a bit of fur in it ... I didn't realise pigs had any fur.'

Furry pigs? The mind boggles. Eventually we arrived in Skegness. At one stage, we had thought we might have all been asked to get out and push his heap of junk, which he called a *taxi*, when it started to spit and splutter, sounding as if it might give up at any moment without warning, but, much to our relief we made it into town.

'Right folks, here we are,' said Kevin as he pulled up. 'The clock tower, a familiar landmark, and if you get lost, ask anyone and they'll point you in the right direction. Would you like to pay me now or shall I add it to your bill?'

'What's the difference?' I asked, with some trepidation.

'Ten pounds. We have to add a small interest charge.'

'What ... thirty percent?' queried Mary, aghast.

'Competitive rates, madam,' came the instant reply.

Talk about r*ip-off* Britain. This was r*ip-off* Skeggie.

'If we call you for a taxi to take us back to the hotel, how much will that be?' I enquired.

'Forty pounds, sir,' replied *rip-off* Kevin.

'Forty quid? It was only thirty to get here, why the difference?' retorted Mick.

'There are no buses back. You can catch a bus in, but you can't get one back.'

'Why the hell didn't you tell us that in the first place?' asked Rose angrily.

'You never asked me. Mr Sleet ordered the taxi ... he didn't ask about any buses.'

'It would be cheaper to walk,' Mary butted in.

'It's a dangerous road and pretty mountainous at various points on the way back,' replied Kevin as he tried to speed off.

'The chiselling bastard. He told us it was only a couple of minutes walk from the hotel to the beach. Didn't he, Mary? He never told us it was an hour and a bloody half by taxi. I bet that Seb Coe bloke could have run with us on his back quicker than Kevin did in his wreck of a taxi,' I was quite incensed now. 'By the way, Alan, how was your breakfast?'

'It would have been nice to have had a bit more,' replied Alan. 'When I went up to choose something, this woman behind the tables told me I could only have one sausage and one piece of fried bread. When I asked her if I could have some bacon with it, she said no. You can have bacon and fried bread, or sausage and fried bread but not all three. Apparently, the tour company doesn't pay them enough money to splash out on a full English. I borrowed Rose's sunglasses and scarf and sneaked off and went round again for the bacon, didn't I, Rose? She looked at me funny like, but couldn't work out who I was, so I got away with it. Was yours the same, Mick?'

'Pretty much, mate. Chris gave me half her fried bread ... said it tasted funny, didn't you luv?'

'It definitely did,' replied Chris. 'I have never

tasted fried bread like that before. I'll certainly be giving that a miss from now on. Ere, is it me, or is it starting to rain?'

'Right, that decides it, then. Wetherspoons sounds good,' I said. 'Its called The Red Lion and, according to my guide, it's on Roman Bank, wherever that is. Come on everyone, let's go before we get soaked through. I'm absolutely famished.'

Chapter 9

Whilst seeking out this Tim Martin lifesaver, it gave our intelligent minds a chance to experience some pleasure in tracing the past history, and to discover the origin and offerings of this seaside town of Skegness. The sky was almost blue, and the air still very fresh, but of the inviting sea and beach there was no sign at all. They were nowhere to be seen.

'The sea must be over there because there are buildings here on this side,' Chris informed us.

'I think she's right,' confirmed Rose. 'It's all smoking over there, could be a load of farmers burning all that stubble stuff.'

A country girl like Rose, could be forgiven for not recognising the, smoking over there, was in actual fact a blanket of sea fog and the reason why the sea was invisible.

'*"This is the most heavenly place I have ever visited. The sun is warm, the sky cloudless and blue, and the sea is calm. Happiness surrounds me with every breeze"*,' I quoted.

'What's that all about, Phil?' Mick asked.

'It's some customer feedback in the hotel brochure, which I picked up at reception on our way out.'

'What a load of bollocks,' said Chris tutting. 'Nothing is cloudless, it's as black as the ace of bloody spades over that hotel ... and it certainly ain't warm. In fact, it's bleedin well freezing. I have never stopped in a place so cold.'

'It was bleeding cold last night. Your teeth, Chris, were chattering away in the glass at the side of our bed, weren't they love?'

'Ere, Mick, for heavens sake don't tell everybody.'

'Sorry, sweetheart. Listen up everyone, they were in the glass but they weren't chattering, were they love?' said Mick, rephrasing his words.

'Who wrote that crap?' enquired Alan.

I turned back to the page, where I'd noticed the comment and replied. 'I don't know, let me see. Hang about, here we are, it's somebody who goes by the name of Hiscock,' and as I looked up, I saw something was puzzling Alan. He was thinking something over in his mind.

'Hiscock ... Hiscock ... yes, Hiscock, that name rings a bell. Now where have I heard that name before?'

'Ere Alan, that bloke back at the hotel, isn't his name Hiscock?' queried Rose, frowning.

'Hmm, I'm not sure, but it could be. Hang about, it says it's from a Mr and Mrs Hiscock. Ere, he ain't married, is he? Surely not, never. Who'd want to marry him? I didn't see any guide dogs in the hotel. Did any of you see one?'

I had noticed earlier when we'd gone downstairs at some ungodly hour, for a so-called apology for a vegetarian breakfast, that Kevin, the porter, was getting rather upfront and personal with something, which looked like it had been dug up by the Time Team, and could only be described, loosely, as a woman with a tash. She was slopping out some object, which looked like something I may have stepped in, in the past, but never had the opportunity to eat. It was what the hotel called, breakfast. Could this behemoth have been Mrs Hiscock? She must be, I thought. Surely he wouldn't have hired a maid that ugly, would he?

'The brochure also mentions the stair carpet,' I added.

'The stair carpet ... what does it say about that?' Alan posed another question.

'Let me see, it says: *"We found the Persian stair carpet, in particular, synonymous with opulence, splendor and beauty. It conjured up the wonder and the magic of, a thousand and one nights, of an Aladdin's cave in the mystical East. I pointed out one tiny hole to the hotel manager, who assured me, that on my return visit, he might offer me a wager to find it, once it has been repaired"*.

'By the way, that reminds me,' interrupted Mick. 'I found a sticker.'

'A sticker? And where was that then?' I queried.

'It was stuck to the stair carpet, and looked as though they'd used it to repair one of the holes.'

I thought that Rose was probably right. The hotel had written the feedback, and in its own brochure. A case of lies, damn lies and The Loss Vagas Hotel Extra.

'What else does it say in the brochure, Phil?'

'Let me have a look ... it says ... oh yes, here it is. *"Hot and cold in every room and see views from all hotel windows".'*

Whoever had written this tripe was, either illiterate because of the misspelling of the word *sea* and the omission of the words *running* and *water*, or they were being completely honest.

'There's never a truer statement,' I added.

'What do you mean, Phil? It's a complete load of bollocks. There's water ... I'll give them that, but it certainly ain't hot, and you can't see the bleedin sea from any window,' said Chris emphatically.

'Ah, but these are the clues. The rooms are whatever, the writer of this trash says they are. They're hot one minute and cold the next. And you can see a view of sorts from the bedroom windows ... at least we could, after I'd cleaned the bloody things,' I replied.

'Bin it, mate,' interrupted Mick. 'Let's walk up through the town, find this Wetherspoons place, and get a decent bite to eat.'

We turned our backs on the town clock and wandered up, what our Hiscock's Guide said, was Lumley Road. I do have to say, though, I found everywhere to be almost litter free. Perhaps the holidaymakers had taken it all to the Costa Del Collapso and Blackpool?

"Look out for a large selection of pavement bistros and the fine dining experiences that are waiting to cater to your every need..." the article continued.

'Are you talking to us, Phil?'

'Sorry, Chris, no. I was reading something aloud from this Hiscock's Guide.'

'Well, does the guide tell you where they are?' queried Mick.

'No, it doesn't, actually. Hang on a minute ... when you turn the page it says... *"Let us know if you can find one"*,' I answered and then did as Mick suggested and binned the brochure.

It was beginning to look like an *I Spy* book of things that cannot be found in Skegness.

We must have been walking for at least half an hour, and passed every type of shop, except one selling food, when Alan suddenly opened up his mouth and said. 'I spy with my little eye something beginning with W.'

'Is it wanker?' piped up Rose.

'Wanker ... what do you mean, wanker?' Alan was looking puzzled.

'Have you spotted Kevin, by any chance, you know, the connoisseur of self-abuse from the hotel?'

'No, you daft bugger. It's Wetherspoons. I've just spotted the Red Lion, it's on the corner just up here ... look,' he replied, pointing up the road.

Alan was right and well spotted. The Red Lion, formerly the Red Lion Hotel, was built circa 1881 by Samuel Clarke, a builder turned publican, hailing from Nottinghamshire. It was at the end of Lumley Road, on the corner with Roman Bank.

Sadly, the large sandstone figure of a lion, which had graced the top of the building was no longer to be seen. It had been removed many years ago, initially to stand on the pavement outside, where children used to sit on him and later, permanently removed from the scene. It is said porters would run across the road to the town's railway station to greet visitors arriving by train, who were staying in the hotel.

'I don't think I will need a lot to eat. I want to save myself for tonight,' said Mary. 'Kevin came up to me after I'd complained and apologised for the poor breakfast. Said he'd make it up to both of us both ... *"Our evening meals are big"* he'd informed me proudly.'

'I bloody hope so, but if this is some sort of a joke, I'll stick that ill-fitting peaked cap of his where he'll need all the experience and skill of a colorectal surgeon to remove it,' announced Mick emphatically.

'I'm looking forward to this. Me and Rose are into double helpings, ain't we gal?' Alan said as he smacked his lips and grinned.

We entered this temple of haute cuisine and looked around for a place where we could all sit together.

'Right. It's coffees all round, then. Grab some seats and I'll go to the bar and order,' I said.

After our coffee stop, we threaded our way back to the seafront. I remember passing the local library but there wasn't a lot to see, even in the way of books. It was full of empty shelves.

The town was all very uniform in appearance. At one point we turned a corner and right there standing in the middle of a roundabout was a church.

'What's that all about then? A church in the middle of a roundabout. Surely they were having a laugh, when they built that, weren't they?' said Chris looking bemused.

'You're probably right,' replied Rose. 'Perhaps a test of faith. I wonder how many people managed to make it on a Sunday morning? According to Kevin, the church is called Saint Matt's and it's got a big organ. He said I should go and have a tinkle on it, if we were passing.'

'We ain't got time for that ... maybe another time. We need to make our way back to the hotel now. We could come back here tomorrow, and Rose can have a tinkle on Matt's organ. We can have a look at the seafront as well, see if the water is any closer to the beach than in Weston,' said Mick.

'I take it from what you've just said, you've been to Weston before?'

'Yes, Phil. Just the once, mind you, and never again. We travelled all the way from Brum to see a load of mud and not much else, didn't we, Chris?'

'I liked them little horse things,' replied Chris.

'What, the donkeys on the beach?' I queried.

'No, not them, those flea-bitten things, I fell off one of them. I liked the ones they had on a little roundabout on the pier. I felt much safer riding on one of them, and the one I was on had a bloody great horn on its face ... didn't it, Mick.'

'Me and Rose went there once,' reminisced Alan. 'I remember the pier, they had a few of those telescope things. Bloody waste of money that was.'

'What was?' asked Mick.

'Those telescope things. I couldn't see any

whales ... I couldn't see any bleedin water. let alone whales.'

'Whales. What do you mean, you couldn't see any whales?'

'I couldn't see any. There was this sign on the one I looked through, which said ... *"Peer here for a peek at Wales"*. They couldn't even spell whales properly. I said to this attendant bloke it's WAILS, and the bloody idiot looked gone out at me. I tell you, I was fuming, and went up to this jobsworth selling entrance tickets to the pier and gave him a piece of my mind. I could have laid one on him, swindling the tourists, like he was. Bloody thing cost me ten bob, it did. I put a tanner in, and after a couple of minutes, it switched off. I thought, I ain't going to see any whales in two minutes, so I kept pumping in the tanners. Rose here got really annoyed with me, didn't you?'

'I certainly did. The swine was spending our bingo money, and when we turned up at the hotel bar later for a session, we discovered we had none left. I told him he was a twat, and it's not a waterpark,' replied Rose, remembering it well.

'Yeah, I thought it was a bit big for a waterpark. I suppose that's why I couldn't see any penguins.'

'What did the bloke who was selling the pier entrance tickets say to you, then?' asked Chris.

'He said I was bloody barmy, and if I didn't behave he'd call the police. I thought it should've been him getting arrested and locked up, not me,' replied Alan huffily.

'Did he not, at least, give your money back?' I

queried.

'No, Phil, he bloody well didn't. No refunds, he said. Told me to go back and have another look, and if I saw any whales to let him know, because he'd never seen any either ... the berk.'

Oh, dear. I thought maybe I'd touched on a raw nerve and dragged up a disappointing memory. My mouth needs to be more careful about what it says.

'Never mind, Alan. You might be able to see a few from the pier, here in Skegness, won't he, Mick?' laughed Chris.

'What's that, sweetheart?'

'Penguins.'

'Oh, yeah. You might be lucky, mate.'

I have to say I was pleasantly surprised to see a leafy suburb, away from the seafront, with tree-lined avenues. It was all very pleasant, and the houses looked very nice. So far, I had not seen anything I disliked, but it was nothing like I'd expected. I was sure I'd see a shopping centre full of chavs. Steer clear of the place on benefits day, I'd been told. Hoever, we saw none of this.

We decided the taxi fare to the hotel was a fare too far, so we set off to walk back. We soon realised that we had been taken for mugs, because the distance from the town to the hotel was not five miles, as we had been led to believe, it was barely a mile and a half. Our taxi driver had taken us around the Wrekin to make us believe we had travelled much further than he had said, so he could justify the extortionate fare we had been charged. How he had managed to live for as long as he had was a complete mystery.

'Will you sod off before I call the police. Yeah, yeah, yeah and up yours too, mate ... sod off,' shouted Kevin as he slammed the telephone back onto its cradle.

'Oh dear, is there a problem? ' I enquired.

'It was one of your bloody lot. He's banging on about there being no hot water in the room. If I've told him once, I've told him a thousand times, the tour operator he booked with hasn't paid us enough money to supply hot water. I told him he can use a kettle, but the idiot's too tight to stump up the non-returnable deposit of fifty quid for the kettle ... tight little bleeder. Now, where was I? Ah yes, Mr Sleet, and what can I do for you?'

'I just wanted to let you know we've arrived back.'

'Oh, really?'

'Yes, really.'

As it happened, I hadn't really wanted to tell him, but after Kevin had cheated us out of so much money for a taxi ride we hadn't needed, and then hearing this moron firing off at another hotel guest, who had the same problem, which I was about to complain of, I thought it wise to keep my mouth firmly shut for the present.

'I've been waiting here all day for a telephone call to come and pick you and your friends up from town, and while I've been waiting for you to call, I've turned down loads of jobs,' huffed Kevin.

It was just another case of lies, and damn lies, but this time it was the Loss Vagas Hotel Extra's manager's lies.

'Oh, and by the way, the name's Street, not Sleet.'

'Street? Thank you Mr Sleet-Street, I will alter our records.'

It took me a while to figure out why the price of a pint of beer was a pound dearer after we'd walked back to the hotel, than it was before we set out. I think maybe it was because Kevin had heard Mick use the phrase *I'm bloody parched,* and Alan saying that he was gasping for a beer.

As the week went by, we discovered the prices of drinks increased exponentially, as the temperatures started to climb outside. Thank God the Loss Vagas Extra Hotel wasn't in the middle of the Arabian bloody Desert.

The mile and a half walk back to the hotel had been a long drawn out and tiring affair but, at least, we had saved the price of a Kev's cab ride. As it turned out, it was a wise decision as we would need the extra money to pay the increased price of the booze. When we had finally got back to the hotel, we were all looking forward to the promised, big evening meal.

The success of the hospitality industry depends largely on the hotel manager. He must have patience, tolerance and kindness. He must know that the best results come from his kind help, and that good food means better service.

'Two slices, is that it? Two slices ... two slices of bread ... and with no butter. Is this the big evening meal you'd promised us this morning? Two pieces of bloody bread.'

'Yes, I told you I'd make it up to both of you,' replied Kevin grinning.

'I want to speak to the bloody manager,' Mary demanded.

'Yes, can I help you?'

'I said, I want to speak to the hotel manager.'

'You are speaking to him, madam,' replied Kevin with a little bow.

'You, the manager. Are you sure you're the manager?'

'I am, yes.'

'Well, you're no bloody good. I might as well speak to a single cell amoeba,' retorted my charming wife, Mary.

'What's one of them, love?' I queried, raising my eyebrows.

'It's a unicellular organism, which can change shape by extending retracting pseudopods, sir.' replied Kevin haughtily.

'You cheeky bleeder. Let me speak to the second-in-command of this dump, then?' demanded Mary.

'That will be my wife, madam. I will get her to come and have a word.'

There is no royal road to success for the hotel manageress. For her, the hotel industry is special in many ways; she ostensibly teaches the great importance of character, and above all, the hotel's success depends on her character, energy, intelligence and her moral worth.

She never came of course. We never expected her

to. We found out the following morning that she had been too busy. Chris reckoned it was because she had been waxing, and said that it looked like the woman's *tash* had suddenly disappeared.

Chapter 10

The hotel's lounge area was nearly full, and the guests were sitting around in very uncomfortable looking armchairs, either reading old newspapers or twiddling their thumbs. Some were swapping stories and shared experiences about the hotel, although none appeared to be complimentary.

Suddenly, the relative calm and quietness was broken by the camp commandant himself, Kevin Hiscock.

'Hello everyone, please can I have your attention. Tonight, there will be a disco in our below stairs entertainment area. If you would care to make your way down to *Kev's Cave* at six o'clock, where there will be a special themed night, and Kev will be playing some popular tunes from a while ago. Looking forward to seeing you all there ... thank you.'

This news was very welcome. I had previously discovered, when I'd pushed back the single curtain at our bedroom window, that it was chucking down with rain, both inside and out. There was enough water on the bedroom floor to float Noah's Arc. I had gone down to reception to report the problem and was told to use the single towel, which we had been provided with on arrival, and block the hole in the window frame. My complaint would be put on a list of jobs for the hotel maintenance man, Kevin, when he felt like getting around to doing them. I was then told I could have another towel at a small charge.

'Let it flow, who cares, I certainly don't. He wants to charge us extra for another towel because we've been told to block the bloody hole up in one of his windows, does he ... the cheeky git,' said Mary in exasperation. 'I've given up moaning about everything, there's no point.'

We made our way into the dining room and met up with Mick and Chris, who seemed to be having a rather heated discussion.

'I thought we'd paid for a day out at Fantasy Island?' Chris was saying to Mick.

'We have,' he replied. 'I had a word with Kevin and he told me the trip had been cancelled. Said the coach roof leaked with all the rain we've had, and he doesn't want to get his arse wet. Said he'd try to arrange a visit on another day, possibly tomorrow, if his seat's dried out. Unfortunately, he also said, there would be an extra charge, because it seems that you cannot change dates at such short notice. Oh, and he asked me to tell you to stop bloody moaning.'

'Are you a man or a bloody mouse? I want our money back,' shouted Chris.

'We can't have it back. He said they don't normally give refunds, and it's written down somewhere in the hotel's rules. Took him a while, but eventually he dug out this piece of paper to show me where it was. I then asked him exactly where it said there would be no monies refunded for circumstances beyond the management's control, and he replied ... *"There ... look, it's in black and white, and as clear as the bloody nose on that silly face of yours"*. He was right as it happened, but I could only see it with the help of a magnifying glass, which he loaned me. Incidentally, I couldn't get a refund on that either.'

'Refund ... on what?'

'The magnifying glass. It cost me a deposit of a fiver just for the loan of it. I've come to the conclusion that we're being ripped off,' replied Mick sounding thoroughly fed up.

'And you've only just realised that. You're too bloody soft, you are,' said Chris shaking her head.

It turned out to be our first day of heavy rain, which was soaking everything. From the early morning to the dewy evening, the pitiless rain poured down in torrents.

I was very tempted to break the mind-blowing monotony, of gazing through the windows of our seaside hell-hole, by donning a pair of bathing trunks, hopping into Kev's cab, and heading for the beach. When I got there, I would dash wildly to the edge and plunge madly into the rainy sea. As if the sea wasn't full up enough already, God Almighty was making certain it got a damn good top-up.

However, I ditched that idea; the ten pound there and twelve pound return fares were the decider, and knowing I would only be marginally less wet walking back from the sea to the hotel in the rain, than I would be after jumping into it, I had to be content with just gazing out on the melancholy view, across a vehicle breaker's yard at the rear of the hotel, and the flat expanse of open farmland beyond.

I remembered with a smile and a feeling of self satisfaction how I had resisted Mary's wish to pay for a room with a sea view. Not, of course, that it really mattered now, because we were nowhere near the sea.

'Poor buggers,' I said turning to Mary.

'Poor buggers, who are the poor buggers?'

'Kevin and his wife, of course, that's who,' I replied with a sigh.

'Why, what's happened to them, then?'

'Nothing ... yet,' I replied. 'It's what is going to happen ... when Chris gets her hands on them.'

'Why's that?'

'She and Mick have paid thirty pounds extra for a room with the privilege of having a sea view. Alan and Rose did the same. There will be blood everywhere. You mark my words.'

Mary and I waited together at reception for Mick and Chris, and Alan and Rose. When they did eventually appear, and after a little conflab, we decided that despite the lousy weather we would all travel together into Skegness on the bus. Kevin had already told us the buses run into town but not the reverse. When we got there, we decided to have a walk along the seafront and catch a bite to eat.

'It's only a quid, but I expect you've all got bus

passes, so it's free,' snarled Kevin.

'Too right, pal,' I said gleefully. 'We're off now ... see you later.'

'You'll be lucky. They don't run on Mondays.'

'What do you mean, they don't run on Mondays? What is they?' I queried.

'The buses. They don't run on Mondays' came the reply.

I was now shaking with rage, and so were the others when I told them.

'Well, I suppose we'll have to get you to take us into town, then,' I muttered crossly, grinding my teeth.

'All six of you, is it?' enquired Kevin, rubbing his hands together.

'Yes, mate. All six of us,' I replied, still grinding my teeth in anger and frustration. Would I have any teeth left at the end of this holiday, I thought to myself.

'Right, that'll be forty pounds, please.'

I wanted to poke the bloke's eyes out. Forty quid. How could he justify a charge as high as that?

'Forty quid? Forty bloody quid? The other day, you said it was only thirty.'

'I know, and it is on all the other days, but not on Mondays. It's a case of supply and demand, you know, and I'm rushed off my feet.'

'*"Don't be a bleedin martyr, luv"*, Mrs Hiscock is always telling me. I provide this service out of the goodness of my own heart, you know.'

'And is it the same fare to return?' I asked, thinking I'd better find out before leaving.

'No ... fifty five quid, including the tip,' replied Kevin grinning.

'Jesus wept ... you bloody...' piped up Rose, angrily.

'You could always walk, then.'

The hospitality industry is dominated by customer service, and hotels can live or die based on customer satisfaction. As guest demands increase, so does the complexity of providing an experience, which satisfies hotel guests. It was, therefore, no surprise to learn that we were not the only inmates, who were less than happy with the service we were receiving, during our period of imprisonment.

'What do mean, *by the sheet*,' a king of comb-overs was at the reception desk asking Kevin. 'I have never stayed in a hotel where you have to buy toilet paper by the sheet. This is absolutely insane.'

This man needs to get out more by the sound of it.

'Will you be wanting one sheet or two, then? I'm sorry, but I have to go; six of our guests are waiting for my taxi. Perhaps, I could refer you to our manageress, if you like?' replied Kevin.

That would be the monster with the moustache. Poor man, he had not realised what he was letting himself in for.

The seafront was very quiet when we all stepped out of the taxi. The Arnold Palmer putting course was empty. Perhaps they were at the nineteenth hole, the clubhouse. I asked if anyone fancied a putt but no one was interested.

'It's pissing down with bloody rain,' said Chris miserably.

I suddenly remembered that years ago while having a lesson at a local golf club with a pro, that he took me to one side and asked if I'd ever fancied playing cricket instead.

Looking across at The Sun Hotel, to where two heavy jacketed smokers were peering across the road into the gloom, I wondered if they were possibly looking for the sun, or perhaps, Wales. Who knows.

We ambled further along the front, passing a Premier Inn and the Fudge Factory, the latter being open but it appeared that there were no takers.

'Anyone fancy a piece of fudge?' I asked.

'Ooh, I shouldn't', replied Chris, giggling, 'I need to watch my weight. '

'Oh, okay then, we'd better give that a miss.'

'Hang about, I was only joking. I wouldn't mind.'

Chris, needing to watch her weight, what was that all about? There was nothing of her to lose.

Rose then decided to accept my invitation. 'That's the trouble with fudge and toffee ... there's nowhere to take them out to swill them if they stick together.'

'Stick what together?' I queried with interest.

'My teeth,' she replied.

It was turning out to be a bit of a bone-chilling dull day until Alan suddenly piped up with, 'I spy with my little eye something beginning with M.'

'Wanker,' laughed Mick.

'Wanker ... what do you mean Wanker ... that begins with a W, not an M,' replied Alan looking a bit confused.

'Wanker may not begin with an M, but Masturbator does,' said Mary butting in.

'Ere, you ain't seen that Kevin bloke driving about in that taxi of his, have you?' asked Rose turning to Alan.

'No, I haven't, you daft buggers, but I've seen a McDonalds. Look, we need to have something to eat, otherwise if we don't, we will die. It's as simple as that. The hotel food is crap, and the service is even worse. I asked that Kevin berk if I could have a serviette last night, and he said I could but there would be an extra charge for it. I told him he must be bloody joking. He then turned round and said, that in that case, I would have to use my hankie instead if I refused to buy one of his poxy serviettes. And then when Rose complained about the taste of the soup, he told her there was nothing wrong with it, because it was only made a week or so ago. She dropped her bread roll on to the floor in shock and it bounced right back up and nearly took a light out before hitting the bloody ceiling.'

'Blimey, so you had the soup, did you?' I asked in amazement. 'What sort of soup was it?'

'I don't know, Phil. It was a funny greenish colour with bits floating on the top.

'This is gastronomic terrorism,' I replied.

'He said that there were no gastros in it, it was pea soup. I told him it was more like piss soup, because that was what it tasted like.'

'If we don't get something to eat,' repeated Alan.

'We will be hunting around for an Oxfam shop or a soup kitchen, so we can get some nourishment. My navel is touching my bloody backbone. I've never been this weight before. My stomach will be thinking my throat's been cut, and they won't recognise me down the pub.'

Alan was right, we needed to get something substantial to eat. McDonald's was not our preferred choice, but there appeared to be little else open, particularly in the way of restaurants.

After all, it was Monday.

Chapter 11

'How the friggin hell are we supposed to ... rip it up ... with all that tripe he's playing?' Mary turned and asked me. 'I haven't heard a single record, which I've recognised up to now, apart from that stupid song by that Donny Osmond kid ... you know the one ... Puppy Love. Did he ever grow up? For Christ's sake, you can't dance to any of that rubbish he's playing; it's too bloody slow.'

'We could always have a smooch,' I replied.

Oh dear, it was that mouth of mine again and this time getting me, not Mick, into trouble. It was now Mary's turn to pull her cardigan together. It was her turn, and not Chris's, to re-adjust her bra straps and give me the pigeon nod. As a member of the unconsidered or negligible sex, commonly known as a mere man, I had never understood when it was the appropriate time to express an opinion, a like, or a need.

'Give over. Ere, don't you be getting any ideas, and that reminds me, we haven't brought any protection with us. Stupid here forgot to pack some,' Mary uttered, looking straight at me.

All of a sudden there was a silence. Chris and Rose

looked at one another, their eyebrows raised as high as they could go, and likewise, their eyes, which were as wide as they had probably ever been. I thought that they might pop out. They looked as though they were about to choke, and I'm pretty sure Mick and Alan already had.

'Protection .. what sort of protection? What do you need protection for, Mary? Surely not at your age,' laughed Chris, her eyes widening even further as she cast a tight-lipped glance at Mick.

''Ere, you ain't got any spare you could let me have, have you?' asked Mary. 'My old man said we won't be getting hot and sticky. *"Take it slow,"* he said. What about you Rose, have you brought any Ultra Shield or Jungle Juice? If you have, can I borrow some, please? I'll give it to you back,' said Mary turning to Rose.

'Borrow ... borrow what, for God's sake?' queried Rose. 'That's disgusting. What have you two been doing? What have you been reading? I've never heard anything like it before in all my life. It's nothing but filth, and I think I'm going to faint now.'

Rose has never heard anything like it before in her life? She needs to get out more.

'What's filthy about Ultra Shield or Jungle Juice? I know it stinks a bit, but what's so filthy about insect repellent? There are flies everywhere in our room; the windows and curtain are crawling with them,' replied Mary, shuddering.

She was right, there was very little in the way of Kev's so-called disco music, which we recognised or, in fact, remembered. There was nothing he had played so far that we, or anyone else, could cut a rug to.

'*Different Drum* by the Stone Ponies ... who the friggin hell are they? I've never heard of them,' shouted Mick above the music.

'Spunky And Our Gang, I've heard of, but I never knew their real name was Spanky And Our Gang,' shouted Chris. '*Give a Damn* ... was that the title of their hit song, then? Have a word with him Mick, will you please, and tell him to play something we all know and can dance to.'

'Yes, mate, you go and have a word, please,' Alan seconded. 'My legs will seize up if I don't start to cut a few shapes and boogie.'

'Alright Alan, just for you, but only because you're a mate,' replied Mick. 'I wish he'd put some bloody lights on, I can't see a bloody thing.'

'Follow the sound, Mick, but be careful not to knock the silly sod over when you bump into him, mind,' said Chris, squeezing Mick's hand, as he disappeared into the darkness with his arms outstretched in front while feeling the way with his hands and fingers.

A short squeal was suddenly heard. 'Ere, get yer bleedin hands off my boobs. Deck him Barry, will you.'

'Sorry luv, it was an honest mistake. I thought I'd bumped into a zeppelin; I reckon I've busted my nose, I have,' said Mick apologising loudly, which told us he was obviously making progress.

When he finally made it back to our table he had a

satisfied grin on his face. 'Sorted...'

'Oh, good, now we're going to get some proper music, then,' said Chris, rubbing her hands together with anticipation.

Imagine the look on Chris's face, when following an invitation to boogie on down, *We'll Meet Again* suddenly came blasting through the darkness. We all looked at each in shock and horror. I found it difficult to understand how Vera Lynn could possibly do anything so evil as to strike us all dumb but she had. That was it, and Mick had just about had enough.

'I said Jeff Lynn, not Vera bloody Lynn, you tosser,' shouted Mick at the DJ.

Immediately a shout came back. 'There's an extra charge for the music of the seventies.'

It wasn't Kev's voice and if it wasn't his I wonder whose it could possibly be. Whatever Mick had said to Disco Kev, it appeared to have had little effect. *We'll Meet Again* was quickly followed by one of my parents' and grandparents' favourites, *Clap Hands Here Comes Charlie*.

'Oh, my God. Who the hell is that?' asked Chris aghast.

'It's a bloke by the name of Charlie Kunz,' I replied. 'My mother and father absolutely loved him.'

'Who the hell is Charlie Kunz when he's at home?' queried Mick.

'He was an American-born musician from the dance band era,' I replied. 'A popular pianist.'

'Clap hands here comes Charlie', was quickly followed by, 'The miner's dream of home'.

'Now you're talking, *The Miner's Dream of Home*, this was one of my mum's all-time favourites,' laughed Rose.

I decided, that if I didn't laugh then I would cry. Disco Kev's cave disco? What a joke, and what an idiot running it. I had thought that this bloke was not the full ticket the moment I saw him suddenly disappear from the coach after first introducing himself. He could have had the word idiot tattooed across his forehead it was that obvious. He appeared to be yet another member of the large and powerful tribe of twats whose influence in human affairs has always been, and always will be, dominant and controlling.

On this occasion his action wasn't limited to any special field of thought, it saturated and regulated the whole. We had already learned that *his word* was the last in everything; his decision was final. When a member of his audience shouted for him to play some decent modern pop music, he responded with *Hurry Up Harry* by Sham 69 - that, said it all.

A woman's dress should be so much an expression of herself, and when seeing it we do not think of the dress but of the woman who is wearing it. The true art of dressing is achieved when it only serves to enhance the charms of a woman and not the wearer. There were a lot of other guests as well as those sitting at tables surrounding the dance floor. The ladies were decked out in all their finery, eyeing one another up, and checking out each other's choice of costume.

'She looks like a pantomime dame. She should be ashamed of herself, the floozy. At her age, I ask you ...

it's disgusting,' I heard one whisper, rather too loudly, to her friend, who was leaning back with her chin tightly drawn into her neck, and she was whispering rather loudly in agreement.

At that moment her husband returned to their table with a pint of beer in one hand and a snowball in the other. Like many of his sex, he was modelling his latest jumper, perhaps an early Christmas present.

'Ere, look at that bloke's jumper,' piped up Mick. 'Rudolph's only got one antler.'

'I noticed that, and if you look carefully, mate, you'll see that Santa's only got one eye,' I replied laughing.

'Yeah, we noticed that, didn't we Rose,' said Chris, grinning.

'Bloody hell, you'd need a pair of steps to climb into them, and a parachute to jump down from them.'

'What are you on about, Mick?'

'The shoes, Chris. Look at the shoes that woman's got on,' replied Mick, raising his eyebrows. 'She looks like she's walking around on a scaffolding tower. Ere, she ain't that Chris Bonnington's wife by any chance, is she? Do you reckon he practiced on her before he climbed Mount Everest?'

If a well-shaped foot is considered to be one of nature's kindest gifts, why is it then, women go out of their way to deconstruct them? There are proportionately more women, who are too short than too tall, and being sensitive to this defect, some try to increase their height with the wearing of high heels. This can make striding uncomfortable, as well as being detrimental to their health.

Other women strive to increase their apparent height by cultivating a narrow waist, but which comes at the expense of shortening the lower limbs, making them appear shorter than they actually are. Some try achieving the same goal by styling their hair high, which often increases the apparent mass of the head, and in turn gives them the appearance of being overweight.

'She could do with losing a lot of weight, she could,' Mary said to me.

'Who, which one?'

'Her over there ... in those blue and green rags. It fits where it touches, that's for sure, but she's wearing heels she can't walk in, and her top is unironed, and it looks as though she's wearing yesterday's meal down her front.'

'It's soup, ain't it? exclaimed Rose.

'Yeah ... tomato by the look of it,' stated Chris with a look of amusement.

'Well ... I do think she's a bit of a looker, though. I love that tattoo on her arm,' said Mick, looking over longingly.

If there was ever a statement, which would stop three women gossiping away, then what Mick had just spouted, had to be it. Poor man, that mouth of his has got him into trouble yet again.

'I beg your pardon. Good looker eh?' Chris turned to Mick giving him the eagle eye.

Blimey, I had never in my life before seen so many cardigans pulled together, so many bra straps adjusted and so many pigeon nods, all at the same time.

'See this girls? This is what I have to put up with all the time. Am I not a good looker then, Michael? You come home at four in the morning ... am I not good looking enough for you anymore? Ere, do you and she know each other, then? Is she one of your Facebook friends, by any chance? Look at her, holding on to that bloke of hers. I bet she's frightened he might run off with something better looking?' berated Chris.

'What, like a goat?'

'Yes, Rose. You got it in one ... like a goat.'

'He sounds like a bit of a beast, then,' said Rose. 'I ask you, coming home at four in the morning.'

Blimey, that early. Poor old Mick, he probably didn't have anywhere else to go?

'It was only an observation,' replied Mick, pleading like a condemned man.

'What do you know about fashion, then? You still wear socks with those bloody sandals of yours,' Chris muttered.

One of the greatest shoe follies of all time must surely be the Chopine, a kind of stiletto, which increased the height of the wearer. They were first worn in Persia and then appeared in Venice some time in the sixteenth century. Their use was encouraged by jealous husbands, who hoped they would keep their wives at home. Chopines were very ornate and the length of the heel could be up to eighteen inches, depending on the rank of the wearer. William Shakespeare even referred to them when he made Hamlet say - *"Your ladyship is nearer heaven than when I last saw you by"*. Fashion is a slavedriver for all those who can read, write, mock and embrace.

Fate ruled that we would enter into the world without the natural covering afforded to lower animals, which protects them from extreme temperatures and the cold. Had it been otherwise, we would have escaped the tyrannical control of the goddess of fashion, and what the French say - *"il faut souffrir pour etre belle"*. Better still, to escape the temptation to wear a jumper with a one-eyed Santa being pulled along by a one-antlered reindeer, and even worse, on a questionable looking sled.

'It looks like a bloody pallet,' Mary said.

'What does?' I queried.

'Santa's sled.

Oh yes, she was certainly right.

Chapter 12

We can define food as any substance that repairs the body's functional waste, increases its growth, and maintains our body heat, along with our muscular and nervous energy. Its ability to do this is best achieved when it is cooked properly.

'Here, let me get my friggin hands on her, I'll bloody kill her, I will,' shouted Mary in a right old state.

'Calm down ... just you calm down. I'll go and have a word with her, leave it to me, and I'll be back in a mo,' soothed Rose trying to calm Mary down.

The *I will be back in a mo* took a bit longer, but eventually Rose returned, and the news was not good. 'Mary, there would be an extra charge.'

'An extra charge? What on earth are you on about? What is *she* on about ... an extra charge? For what ... cooking a pork bloody chop?'

'Yes, that's what she told me. There is an extra charge if you want it cooked,' replied Rose apologetically.

'You have to be bloody joking ... a pork bloody chop cannot be eaten raw. You'll get a bloody tapeworm or die of food poisoning,' shouted Mary.

As I watched the drama unfolding I thought back to the message greeting, which was hanging on the wall behind reception - *More dreams are realised in our hotel than in any other hotel in England*. Obviously, dreams of a cooked pork chop had not been one of them. I was beginning to understand what the word *Extra* meant in the hotel's name. It would seem to appear that there was an extra charge for nigh on anything and everything. I stood up and walked over, with the plate on which a raw pork chop was breathing its last, to the woman standing behind the row of picnic tables where there were three trays and a stack of plates. I won't use the word chef, because that implies he or she is a competent and knowledgeable cook. The rather strange-looking lady who was, by now, minus her tash, and tapping a large ladle on the top of one of the tables in time with a tune, which must be playing in her head and that only she could hear.

'Excuse me. My wife would like a pork chop that has been cooked.'

The so-called chef de cuisine cast me a quizzical and most disagreeable look.

'I can't help that,' said the spud chipper. 'Your wife should have ordered one then, shouldn't she? I can't cook it now as our gas bottle has just run out, and we'll not be getting a full one until Wednesday.'

'Hang about, are you are telling me if you want something cooked for breakfast, then you have to order it beforehand?' I queried.

'No, I didn't say that. I said if it's something extra

for breakfast, which in this case is cooking, then she must order it well in advance,' replied the chipper.

'May I remind you,' I retorted. 'I did order my wife a pork chop for breakfast. I filled in the necessary form, which is at the side of our bed, and brought it down to reception and handed it over the counter to your husband. I did all the right things; I followed the rules. And regardless of that, the customer is king.'

'No, you didn't.'

'Yes, I damn well did.'

'No. you damn well didn't,' she countered. 'You didn't tick the *would you like it cooked* box. That's what you forgot to do, and it's through your wilful neglect as a loving husband that your wife got a raw pork chop. Is she a queen and are you a king? No, I think not.'

This was getting ridiculous.

'There wasn't a w*ould you like it cooked* box to tick,' I replied, trying to hold back my rising temper.

'Yes, there is,' the tashless woman replied emphatically.

'Yes, there is? No there bloody well isn't? Where the bloody hell is this w*ould you like it cooked* box, then?' I yelled back.

I was getting really angry listening to all this nonsense, and mourning the fact, that at some stage in my life, I'd been offered an Anger Management Course, but had declined to go on it. I will never need it, I'd remembered thinking to myself. Unfortunately, I needed it now.

'It's on page ten of the Extras booklet at the side of

the bed. There is one in every room,' the spud chipper replied. 'You ordered the pork chop on page three, but forgot to tick the *would you like it cooked* box on page ten.

'Page ten?'

'Yes, page ten of fifteen. It's quite easy you know. I presume you can read ... kings and queens usually can ... can't they?'

With the meagre food portions, there was no chance to escape the evils of moderation, unless one were to eat an uncooked pork chop. Then one might, with a bit of luck, end up in a hospital bed where they would be assured of at least three decent cooked meals each day for the duration of their stay.

Chapter 13

'Calm down, Phil. You need to calm it and just try and put it behind you. Don't let it spoil our day out.'

I knew that what Mick and Chris were urging me to do was exactly that, to calm down, and the right thing, but it was still gnawing at me. It was difficult for me to suppress the urge not to just go and press some nerves in both Mr and Mrs His..bloody..cocks' necks. This was, of course, if I could persuade Mary to let me jump ahead of her, and her pork chop, in the queue.

'What does NO TH PARAD mean, Phil?' asked Chris from behind.

'Er, there are a couple of letters missing,' I replied looking up. 'It should read North Parade.'

'Oh, right. I thought it was foreign or something. Yes, I see it now ... North Parade Bingo Club.'

'I saw that Shirley woman, the one who was sobbing on the bus ... you know, the one who lost her mum. I saw her this morning on our way out,' said Rose. 'Well, she wasn't sobbing then; she had smiles all over her face, the nasty piece of work. Her husband told me her name had been picked out of the hat for free entrance, to tonight's bingo at the hotel. When I asked him what he and his wife were doing today, he said she'd won a tenner on a scratch card, and that's where they were off to.'

'What, the North Parade Bingo Club?' queried Chris.

'No, back to WH Smiths ... they're going to buy a newspaper with her winnings ... lucky cow,' replied Rose. 'You have to pay an extra charge, on top of the price, for a newspaper in the hotel. Kevin said it was a delivery charge; it's dearer than the paper itself.'

We walked a little further on to *The Seaview*, which was advertised as a family pub, and we decided to stop here to buy a hot drink, sit down and rest our tired feet. We could look across the large car park opposite and admire the unobstructed view of the sea.

There is something about coastal towns, such as Skegness, which make them more attractive to those further inland. When one gets to know the town and its surroundings, its like becoming conversant with someone; like the process of falling in love, as ultimate as it is quick. You may leave and not return until many years later, but when you do there is still the unchanged shoreline, the daintiness and quiet. The remoteness and the hoped for childish certainty that the friendships you made, will still be there waiting for you.

A city is more varied and striking, and after a fashion more imaginative, almost poetic. It offers more financial and social variation, but that is where the comparisons end, and in such a dramatic way, for the pulling power of the sea is far greater than the pulling power of the city.

I had finally managed to calm the anger I'd felt at breakfast, and raw pork chops were no longer an issue. Mr and Mrs Hiscock were set to live for at least another twenty-four hours.

This Skegness of my childhood dreams was very quiet, and there was hardly a soul about. We saw nothing of, what could be described as a crowd, it was amazing, far-flung, and almost dead. I had talked to a friend before our week away and he had assured me that Skegness had greatly improved since my childhood visit. He told me there had been great alterations to the seafront, and with a gentler type of person to be seen parading along the pier. I had taken him at his word and so wanted to see it for myself. 'The lying swine,' I muttered under my breath.

'Who's that?' queried Alan.

'My mate, Steve Bird.'

'What's he been lying to you about, then?'

'He told me I would still be able to see middle-class matrons from Banbury, looking all of their sixty years, walking up and down with their sixty-plus-year-old husbands. They would be serenading up and down the pier. But they're nowhere to be seen. Look, all you can see are the tattooed gum chewers. Take a look at that one over there, she's got more tattoos than they've got in the Royal Navy. Who the hell is SEYEMON ... the idiot who pricked her couldn't even spell.'

We had arrived at the pier, but it bore no resemblance to the one I had remembered from all those years ago. Half of it had disappeared, and now instead of cabins selling sticks of rock, cups engraved with amusing characters and seaside trinkets, all that we could find was an amusement arcade, a Hollywood bar - whatever that was - and a bowling alley.

'Look at that, Mick,' said Chris in amazement.

'Look at what?'

'On the side of that building.'

'Which building?' asked Mick, looking a bit confused.

'Over there, the Beachside Tavern ... look at the picture painted on the side of it. It's like one of those saucy seaside postcards.'

'Yeah, so it does. What does it say?'

'It says... *"What is the shortest sentence in the English dictionary but the longest sentence in your life"*,' replied Chris, reading out the wording.

'I don't know,' Mick said baffled. 'What does it mean?'

'I do.'

'I do what?'

'Yeah, what do you do then, Chris?' queried Rose as well.

'I do nothing. I ain't done nothing,' replied Chris knowingly.

'It doesn't make any sense,' chipped in Alan.

'If I'd been married for fifty years, I still wouldn't have a bleedin clue. Come on luv, own up and put us out our misery. What have you done?' pleaded Mick.

'Nothing,' was the reply.

Right, at long last we had finally got that argument sorted out.

'I'm hungry,' I announced. 'I think we ought to wend our way back to that Red Lion nosh house and stock up. Tonight's menu back at the hovel doesn't look at all appealing.'

'Why's that then, Phil?' enquired Mary.

'Did you not read what it said at the entrance to that so-called restaurant of theirs?'

'No, what did it say?'

'Cold buffet.'

'Oh, yes. I remember now. They've run out of gas bottles, and they won't be getting another delivery for a few days.'

'Phil's right everyone,' said Mick. 'Let's go and get stuffed.'

Chapter 14

The warning sign was there as soon as the word bingo had been mentioned. I knew there would be problems aplenty.

The game of *bingo* originated in Italy, apparently. It originates from, *Il Gioco del Lotto d'Italia*, an Italian lottery, and bears no resemblance to the game, which was to be played later in the hotel's entertainment room, while we would be sitting quietly sucking our drinks through straws in the bar.

The bingo game in the Loss Vagas Extra Hotel would differ in one important way. All the numbers between one and fifty, used in the Italian version, would be used on this occasion, but with one exception. I was pretty sure that the number twenty would not be one of them. The major difference between the Italian and the Loss Vagas Hotel Extra versions, would be the introduction of a pugilistic element. It had all the potential for turning nasty and violent, particularly if someone found out that the number twenty was missing from Kevin's collection of balls.

'We will not be going to the bingo tonight,' I announced to the others, while Mary was upstairs perming her ears and getting ready. 'When I checked out the broken leg on our bed the other day, I saw that someone had scratched the words *"there ain't no number twentee"* into the edge of the wooden frame. I reckon the bingo is going to be nothing but a stitch-up, and nobody will win. I wouldn't mind betting that every bingo card will have the number twenty printed on it, but there'll be no chance of getting a full house. You mark my words.'

'Hee, hee, hee ... so that sobbing Shirley cow ain't going to win a penny then.' Rose laughed out loud. 'Ere, I might win instead.'

'It could be me?' piped up Chris.

'Yes, it could be,' answered Mick. 'It's an even chance, and Mary could even win.'

'Not unless she has a number twenty on her card, mate,' I said.

'Do you honestly think, that that Kevin bloke would stoop so low as to play such a dirty trick on us all?' asked Alan, his eyebrows shooting up incredulously.

'Well, Alan,' I replied. 'When I take all things into consideration, and think back to our experience with the bus, the taxi, the raw pork chop, the deposit required to use the magnifying glass, the extra charge for the soap, the additional towel, which never materialised even though I'd paid for it, the crappy disco music, and so on ... then the answer has to be yes. That bastard would do anything to turn a buck. He's the type who would pick a kid's pocket and pinch a charity box from the Post Office. Mary and I have decided that we will not want to risk having our blood spilled, by buying into the bingo scam. We will retreat to the bar for an extortionately overpriced drink. Incidentally, it's my choice of drink tonight. We are going to share a pint of beer, and I've kept the two straws from last night's Babycham. I was told that Kevin's wise to our little game and that he was up for most of the night hunting for those two straws.'

'Why would he be doing a thing like that, Phil?' queried Mick.

'He doesn't want people sharing drinks. He wants everyone to buy one each.'

We lined up and edged our way into the dining room. The first thing that caught my eye was a large bowl of lettuce. Next to this was a small bowl of cucumber and to the side an even smaller bowl of cherry tomatoes.

'Right folks, what would you like?' asked the disher-outer. 'We have a choice of lettuce, cucumber or tomatoes.'

'I would like some of each, please,' said the lady in front of us.

'Sorry madam, but I think you misunderstood what I said. What I actually asked, was that you have a choice of one of the three. I did not say some of each ... next.'

I could hardly wait for my turn, because I too had a question I needed an answer to.

'Yes sir. How may I help you?'

'I would like some of each as well, please,' I said looking her straight in the eye.

'I'm sorry sir, but....'

'Yes, yes, yes,' I cut her off short. 'I heard all that tripe. I want some of each, and if I don't get some of each, then somebody's blood will get spilled and it won't be mine.'

'I see,' came the reply. 'So, I take it you won't be having the jam roly-poly for pudding, then.'

'And, why am I not having the jam roly-bloody-poly pudding, then?' I queried, raising my eyebrows.

'Because you cannot have both. I know what you're going to say,' replied the disher-outer, raising her hands. 'I must remind you that it is written down in the hotel's information book ... under the Code of Conduct section; Section Two, lines four and five. I can read it to you, that is, if you have a reading problem.'

'So, this is it, is it? This is all we are going to get, then?'

'No, we have salt and pepper over there, and loads more on the table at the end,' she replied, pointing with a suspect grubby finger.

Where the hell she had poked that digit, God only knew, I thought.

'Loads more of what?' I enquired.

'Salt and pepper.'

It appeared, that if you didn't like salt or pepper, you had a major problem. What a good idea it had been to fill up as we had on previous days, with a meal from Tim Martin's temple of haute cuisine, The Red Lion. I put my dinner plate back on the pile, and walked back to our table.

'Come on Mary. It's time for us to make a move ...

trouble is brewing. I've just heard some bloke shouting about having to pay extra for a spoonful of sugar, and that Hiscock woman is shouting back at him about their hotel having a five-star rating.'

Five-star? I had obviously misheard something? Surely that should have been a five-scar rating. I had noticed as we walked into the dining room that the suggestions box behind the reception desk was, in actual fact, a paper shredder.

'Rose and I will catch you lot up,' said Alan as we were departing. 'She's using all her charm to negotiate on an extra lettuce leaf. I'm sure that bastard used a sleight of hand. When I asked her for a tomato, I saw her put one on my plate, but when I got back to our table the bloody thing wasn't there. I reckon she could be the magician they've advertised for the show tomorrow night.'

'A magician tomorrow night? How do you know that?' Chris enquired of Alan.

'That Kevin bloke told me earlier on when I passed him in reception, that he's also organised a quiz night. Told me about the Great Whodeani, and how he could pick people's pockets, and then pointing to the hotel notice board, he advised me to watch my wallet. *"We have notices all over the hotel,"* he said.'

'We've got one in our bedroom, haven't we Mick,' said Chris nodding.

'So have we,' I said.

'I told him it was strange, because I hadn't heard a Brummie accent about the hotel, other than yours and Mick's,' Alan said to us.

'Is Kevin a Brummie then?' I queried. 'What did he reply when you told him that, Alan?'

'He just tapped his nose, and walked off.'

'A quiz night? I really fancy a go at that,' I said to Mary as we made our way into the bar area, but as we were passing reception we were stopped by the man himself, Kevin.

'No bingo tonight folks?' he asked us. 'Will you be having some drinks instead, then?'

'Yes, we will. Is there an extra charge depending on where we sit in the bar area?' I enquired sarcastically.

'We do get some jolly japers,' he laughed.

I noticed he was looking closely at my jacket pockets, and Mary's handbag as we walked away. On entering the bar area we found the six of us could sit at any table we liked. There was no one else in there, and it appeared that every other guest was partaking in the game of bingo.

'That Kevin bloke was giving you a funny look, wasn't he, Phil. Why do you think he was doing that, mate?' Mick asked as we sat down.

'He was looking to see if we had any straws,' I replied. 'Which reminds me, Mick, that when I come back from the bar, I want you and Chris to sit close together, obstruct his view, so he can't see me and Mary sucking through our straws. I've been told that customers are not allowed to share drinks. It's against hotel policy, apparently; some bollocks about health and hygiene.'

In the field of ethics, three people are more likely

to have the greatest influence on the whole of humanity than any other - the philosopher, the politician and the bingo caller. Now under normal circumstances, there are not many things, which either the politician or the philosopher would ever be able to agree on with each other. However, I am not talking about normal circumstances. In the natural order of events, there is one thing they will both agree on, and that they will both recognise. They know a cheat when they see one.

An enormous roar with boos and shouts of fix, signalled the end of the bingo. We waited with interest to hear what had gone on and find out who, if anyone, had won anything at all. Guests were being made to line up at the entrance to the bar and the men were asked to turn out their pockets and the ladies told to make their handbags available for inspection.

'What's all that rigmarole about?' asked Chris frowning. 'I wouldn't let anyone look in my handbag, not even my Mick. I'd skin him alive, I would.'

'Perhaps they've had a bomb scare or summat,' piped up Mick. 'Look at that woman over there. Ere it's Shirley and she's shaking and sobbing her heart out.'

'A bomb scare? The hotel is worse than any I've seen on the telly that's been bombed. It would be a waste of explosives sticking one in here,' said Alan guffawing.

'Calm down mate,' I soothed. 'Kevin is only looking to see if he can find some hidden straws.'

Poor lady; poor, poor lady. I have to say I did feel

sorry for Shirley when I discovered that misery had been piled upon misery. Not only had she lost her mum, it now appeared she had missed out on a jackpot as well. Poor, poor woman.

'All I wanted was number twenty for a full house,' I could hear her sobbing.

'Never mind luv,' her kind and loving husband, Barry, was trying to console her. 'I'll treat you to another scratch card tomorrow and, who knows, you might win another tenner. I could kill that bastard for upsetting my missus like that.'

Chapter 15

It doesn't seem to matter how many times you rub and stroke a towel across your adductor magnus, your pubofemoral portion, or that ischiocongylar bit in your rear end, you will discover it is still near enough soaking bloody wet by the time you have untangled and tugged a pair of underpants from the chest of drawers in your bedroom and dragged them up your legs. How frustrating is that?

Today my frustration was made even more frustrating when, as I woke up, I suddenly remembered today was Mary's turn to use the single towel we had been given at the start. Worse still, I was up and about, and raring to go but she was still fast asleep and giving it her all by attempting to snore her nose off. The earplugs, which had been kindly supplied to us both, for an extra charge, I might add, seemed to make not an iota of difference.

I was still woken up in the middle of the night by a rendition of something, which sounded very much like the *Frog Song*. I don't know who was providing the *bom-bom bom*, or the *sink-or-swim* beat, but I had a mind, to sink him or her, if I could find out who. The words - *"Oh, yes mate, you will be needing them alright.*

The walls here are paper bloody thin. How many ... two sets, is it? That will be four quid, please" were coming back to haunt me, and top of my list of people to kill, was the idiot who, with a choice of eighty-eight notes, decided that a B Flat Minor would have the desired effect and wake up all the guests. Every bloody time, whoever it was, made the ceiling bend. I kept thinking that the flippin *la-la-la* would crack the only pane of undamaged glass in the bedroom window.

Talking of which, when I looked out of it I saw it had finally stopped raining and the driver's seat on the coach must surely have dried out sufficiently, for us all to go on one of the organised, Days Out, which we had already booked. Sadly, it would not be to Fantasy Island as this had been scrapped altogether, and as a result, Kevin had assured everyone we would all be given a cash refund.

'Where are we going, then?' Mary asked me.

'I have no idea.'

'Rose and I have been told it's going to be a Mystery Tour, haven't we Rose?'

'We have, Mary, and I'm looking forward to it.'

'I heard someone talking about us going to Gibraltar,' interrupted Mick.

'Blimey, that's foreign, ain't it? I've heard of it, it's abroad somewhere. Ere, I didn't pack our passports.' Chris said to us all.

The town of Gibraltar is built on a bed of red sand. The houses are built with different materials, mainly a strong, well-soaked cement called Tapia; many of them are plastered and coloured on the outside, to limit the intense rays of the sun. Some are tiled, but the flat terraced roofs in the Spanish homes remain, and on many verandahs and towers, the inhabitants can, without leaving their homes, bask in a bright perspective.

The prospects of a mystery tour to Gibraltar, of all places, seemed to lift everyone's spirits. Everywhere I looked I could see happy smiling faces, and I could hear lots of chattering and laughter. One of our group was looking intently into a phrase book and practising whatever it was that he was reading to his wife.

'Oiy yoo-oh, uno ... no, er sorry ... dos des lunettes Sangria, poor per for. Vielen danke. That should do the trick?' I heard him say.

'Ere, Alan. Can you speak any of those foreign words? If so, what is "*I'm busting for the bog*" in Spanish ... just in case we need to ask.'

'I don't know, Rose. Do you know Phil?' said Alan turning to me.

'I haven't a clue, mate. You'll just have to, serre tes joues ensemble,' I replied.

'What does that mean, then?'

'I don't know what it is in Spanish, but in French it translates to "*squeeze your cheeks together*".'

A holiday in Skegness does not often include a trip to Spain and the British Overseas Territory of Gibraltar. In fact, our trip today could be the first time it had ever happened?

Although it is connected to Spain, Gibraltar is not a part of Spain; it belongs to us here in England, and for those who wish to maintain unity in their memories of a country and a people, the garrison and fortress are not in colour with the Kingdom of the Moors. It is not an easy place to get to, standing out as it does but, with its feet still in the water, this mighty rock was once known as one of the Pillars of Hercules. Aeons ago, the pillars marked the edge, and end of the world. Where the waters of the Atlantic mingled with those of the Mediterranean.

'Hurry up folks, this way, the coach is waiting. We will need to get back early for the Loss Vagas Hotel Extra's magic show this evening with the Great Whodeani. Thank you,' shouted our driver, Kevin.

After a torturous, metal on metal crunching sound, the engine of the coach fired into action. When Kevin finally discovered which gear was which, we were off. It was slow at first, but after a few miles we were zipping along like the Dukes of Hazzard at a breakneck speed of twenty miles an hour. I say breakneck, because there was a real chance that it might have happened to any one of us, if we hadn't decided to support our necks throughout the journey. It felt as though the coach had no suspension.

I often find that the last taste is the sweetest; that only when you have come to know a place, can you fully enjoy it, after you've managed to obtain its freedom. Wandering around, or sitting for a while under a shady tree, or looking upon the swaying cornfields, you feel as though you are master of the situation. The countryside around our hotel was flat and uninteresting. Two people sitting in front of myself and Mary were obviously thinking the same.

They were reminiscing about the honeymoon they had taken in Skegness many years ago.

'Do you remember our honeymoon, sweetheart?' the woman's husband asked, as he looked adoringly at her. 'When we arrived the other day, I thought, bloody hell, this is the hotel we stayed in all those years ago. It ain't much different from what it was back then. In fact, I don't think it's changed at all. The dodgy stair carpet is still the same, the one I'd tripped on and twisted my ankle, and spent four days in bed with my leg up on an extra pillow, which we'd had to pay for.

Can you remember the *"I shagged Dwayne here"* message, which was scrawled on the wall by the lift's entrance? That's still there, and the lift wasn't working then either. The management has changed mind you. Well, that Kevin bloke is new, but I don't know about the woman, who slops out the evening meals. I'm sure she was here all those years ago ... I recognised her moustache.'

'I'm sure you're right Fred, replied his wife. 'I thought I recognised her but she didn't have a moustache back then, did she? The food's the same though, and they still have the bingo night and the disco. They're even playing the same records; Vera Lynn brought back so many memories.'

'I'm sure you're right,' said Fred. 'Can you remember our first night together sweetheart ... how we made mad passionate love, and can you remember the first words you said to me afterwards?'

'Oh, I can my love. How could I ever forget?' his loving wife replied.

'Will you remind me then, just one more time sweetheart, please?'

'I will never forget it. I said we ain't painting our bedroom ceiling that friggin yellow colour, no way.'

'I remember now,' said Fred to his loving wife. 'I thought you'd said magnolia, and whenever magnolia is mentioned I always get a tingling feeling and I can't go into B&Q, without breaking into a sweat. Do you remember when our Barry was born, and the doctor said he had to be circus sized?'

'Yes, I do my love. He was just a few days old, wasn't he? Poor little bleeder, it must have hurt him so much because he couldn't walk for the next fifteen months.'

I never got to hear about their Tracy and her wobbly bits because suddenly the coach ground to a halt.

'Why are we stopping here?' queried Chris. 'There's bugger all around. They usually stop at some roadside services for a break, but we've only been going for about an hour. He'll be late for the ferry and we'll miss our slot. Ere, I ain't sleeping on this bleedin coach all the way to Gibraltar.'

'Right folks, can I have your attention, please,' announced Kevin. 'We have arrived at our destination. Can you be back here at this spot in four hours, please when I will return with the coach to pick you all up. I usually stop here myself, but I ain't paying them Pay and Display prices. They've rocketed and it's a bleedin rip-off.'

Well, Kevin certainly knows all about rip-offs. It

takes a ripoff merchant to know a rip-off when he sees one.

We rose to our feet, shuffled along the central aisle, and in turn stepped down from the coach straight into a thick blanket of fog. The six of us walked slowly across a large parking area to a fence, where we stopped to survey our surroundings.

'Is this it?' queried Rose, looking through the gloom. 'I can't see sod all in this fog.'

'Yeah, looks like it,' replied Chris. 'Is this all there is ... where's all the shops? I want to get myself a new handbag and a couple of bottles of liqueur to take back home. Where's that bloody great rock thing, then? Has it been pulled down or something.'

'It looks like it,' answered Mick. 'They're knocking everything down these days. You'll just have to wait until the fog lifts to see what's been built in its place. It's probably yet another warehouse ... they're building them everywhere.'

'I have just noticed some sort of information board over the other side of the car park,' I said to the others. 'I'm going to walk over and see what it says. I won't be long.'

Mary and I walked across the parking area, which, incidentally, was devoid of cars. The large information board was similar to the ones, which can be found at places of interest. The first thing I saw was the words Heritage Coast followed by Gibraltar Point National Nature Reserve Visitor Centre. Mary and I turned and looked at each other.

'Will you tell them, or shall I?' I asked her.

'What ... that Kevin has taken a wrong turning and we're not where Chris and Mick and Rose and Alan thought we were going? That there are no handbag shops or duty-free? There will be blood spilled, you know.'

Gibraltar Point is a stretch of unspoiled coast that runs southwards from Skegness, to the mouth of The Wash, and according to the visitor's information board, an area of outstanding beauty.

'I have never been known to swear and I won't lower myself to do so in this instance, but if I ever get my bleedin hands on him, I'll friggin well kill him. What do you mean it ran out of ink? What is it that ran out of bloody ink?' shouted a fat man in socks and sandals.

Oh, dear. Another unhappy traveller who appeared determined to get on the list of those who would like to assist our leader in shuffling from this mortal coil. It appears that Kevin's permanent marker pen had decided to run out of permanent ink before he could finish writing the details of today's trip on the hotel notice board. To make matters even worse, as if they could get any worse, there was an extra charge he had been unable to add to the post. This *extra* was a payment required for the return journey to the hotel.

'I have never heard the word *murder* used so many times, Mick,' said Chris turning to him.

'You're right there, I haven't either,' said Mick scratching his head. 'I thought it a bit odd, that when we got here, there weren't any shops selling sombreros and them donkey things. You know, like the one I brought back from Ibiza for you.'

'Yes, I remember. Oh, the memories are flooding back now. Do you remember I nearly poked my eye out? That was when we were courting all those years ago. Pity that Spanish chap couldn't spell my name right when he tattooed it on your arm,' said Chris laughing.

A tattoo on Mick's arm?

'What was wrong with the tattoo then, mate,' asked Alan being inquisitive.

'The greasy idiot couldn't spell, could he. I told him what Chris's name was, and I even wrote it down on my arm for him, exactly where I wanted it pricked. Clisteen ... I ask you. I could have strangled him there and then. *"It's only got one e, matey, not two,"* I'd shouted at him ... the bloody berk.'

Chapter 16

The word magic itself has a seductive sound and its practice as an art form will probably never lose its appeal to people's minds. Magic originally meant priestly, and it's likely that the word is very ancient, having been handed down to us by the Greeks and Romans, who had received it from the Persians. In turn, the Persians owe it to the Babylonians, the Babylonians to the Assyrians, and the Assyrians to the Sumero Akkadians.

As arranged, Mary and I met up with Mick, Chris, Alan and Rose in the reception area after yet another disappointing evening meal.

'How was your fish and chips, Mick?' I asked.

'They would have been a lot better if they'd been cooked. I forgot to tick the box.'

He was right, they would have been a lot better cooked, but if you don't remember to tick the box they will be served raw.

'And how was yours, Chris?' enquired Mary.

'Well, put it this way, it's the first time I've tasted cooked melon. When Kevin's missus put it down in front of me the only thing I recognised was the bowl. It was just a load of sludge with a cherry and some skin floating on the top.'

Chris had also fallen into a similar trap by asking for her melon not to be cooked.

'Our prawn cocktail was the same, wasn't it Rose?' said Alan. 'This bloke told me he saw a chap in a mask looking into one of the dustbins out the back this morning; stopped and asked him what he was doing and the chap replied that he was treating the dustbins for ulcers. I knew he was joking, but I wouldn't be at all surprised if he was.'

It's unbelievable what a dustbin at the Loss Vagas Hotel Extra has to put up with. All they ever do is just stand there.

We all walked down the flight of steps into the entertainment area, which was pitch black. The only thing I could make out at first were fellow guests shuffling around with their arms outstretched, feeling their way around, and some were stumbling over chairs. It was like something out of Shaun of the Dead.

'It's bloody dark in here. Mary, can you turn on the torch on your iPhone, please? I can't see a bloody thing.'

'I would, Phil, if I could find it, but it's so dark I can't see my bleedin handbag.'

'It's round your neck.'

'I know, but I can't see the zip to open it.'

'Alan, where are you mate, can you hear me?'

'Yes, Phil. I can hear you, but I can't see you. Where in hell are you? Ere hang about ... what the…'

'Ere you, pack it in will yer. Jim, bottle this bloke will yer, he's groping my boobs,' shouted an invisible woman.

'I would, Edna love, if I could see him.'

'Ere, there he goes again. Get off, you friggin pervert. Here, take a load of this.'

Suddenly there was a scream, but who was it? It was impossible to say, but I was soon to discover.

'Oiy, you friggin cow. What was that for?'

It was Chris's voice. She had been on the receiving end of something padded, which was covered in faux leather.

'Mick, some tart's just hit me with her handbag. Wallop her, will you?' shouted Chris.

'I'd love to, that is, if I could see her.'

Suddenly a blinding spotlight was turned on, which was directed onto a black curtain hanging across the front of a small stage. People were rubbing their eyes and shielding them from the blinding light. Out of the corner of my eye, I could see a man using a type of practised yoga move to examine a tear in the seat of his trousers.

'These are my best friggin trousers,' he hmphed, turning to his wife. 'It's that bloody chair I just sat on, someone's put superglue on the bloody seat.'

'I think it might be custard?' his wife replied. 'Careful, I don't want you being accused of nicking one of their chairs, and I certainly don't want Kevin seeing you walking away with one of his chairs stuck to your arse.'

Suddenly, a microphone made a screeching sound and the Great Whodeani, looking suspiciously like our hotel manager, Kevin, burst through the curtains.

Whether by design, or misjudgement, he then sort of toppled off the stage and landed on the floor in front of a few of the guests who had considered themselves brave enough to sit up close to the action, and have a chance to see if they could work out how The Great Whodeani performed his magic tricks. In a cloud of pigeon feathers he sprang to his feet, and readjusted his tie, and the black wig, which had slipped down in front of his eyes.

'Good evening everyone, let the show begin,' he shouted in a sort of mid Atlantic accent.

What then followed was both pitiful and painful. It was an insult to all those professional magicians, who are members of the Magic Circle.

First off, there was the failed card trick. Even though every card in the pack, which The Great Whodeani was holding in his hand, was the eight of spades, he argued with a lady in the audience, whom he'd invited to take a card from his pack, that the card she had chosen was the queen of hearts.

'It looks bugger all like the queen of hearts to me, it's the eight of bloody spades,' protested the woman.

This was followed by the production of The Great Whodeani's magic matchbox, in which the magician said he'd already written the answer to a list of questions he would ask a member of the audience. I had to admit I was rather intrigued by this one. So much so, in fact, that I urged Mary, Alan, Rose, Mick and Chris to wait until we had seen it before escaping for an extortionately priced drink at the bar.

The Great Whodeani chose his victim from one of

those sitting in the front row. 'Madam, I am inviting you to think of a number below ten.'

The willing victim told him she had, and asked if he would like to know what number it was.

'No ... no,' he replied. 'This is all part of the trick. I now want you to double the number and then add six to it.'

'Yes, I've done that, so would you like to know what it is now, then?'

'No, no, no ... how many times have I got to tell you, you stupid tart. Er, sorry ... you lovely lady. No, it's all part of the bleedin trick, madam. Now please concentrate.'

'I am concentrating,' she replied.

'This is the difficult bit now. Halve your answer, take away the first number you thought of, and tell me what number you have, please?'

'I can't. You told me not to tell you,' came the reply.

'Yes, I know I did earlier, but now I want you to tell me the number you've arrived at, please?'

'Oh, I don't know as though I should,' she replied turning to her husband sitting beside her. 'What do you reckon, Fred?'

'Will you just tell me the number, you silly old bat ... please?' The Great Whodeani asked through gritted teeth.

I have to admire people who have the ability to wind other people up. Whether it was a natural ability or not, the lady had done a good job in doing so.

'Oh, all right, then,' replied the lady. 'Fred said for

Christ's sake tell him so we can bugger off to the bar. The number is three.'

'Is it really, The Great Whodeani said. Are you sure?'

'Of course I'm sure you stupid twat.'

'Well, in that case, if you'd like to take this matchbox, open it up and remove the piece of paper from inside and then read the message out loud so the rest of the audience can hear. Tell them all what I've written down, please,' said The Great Whodeani with a wave of his arms.

Taking up the offer to open the matchbox, the woman pulled out a small piece of paper. 'Oh my God, Fred ... he's right. I told him my number was a three, and he's written down the word CORRECT. I would never have believed it.'

'I would like to teach that idiot how to swallow a sword, given half the chance,' her husband, Fred, was heard to say. 'I might even go out and buy one myself.'

As suddenly as the lights went out they came back on. However, they were out long enough for someone to pinch someone else's pint of beer.

'Ere, call the police, some tosser's nicked my cheese and onion crisps,' someone shouted.

Kevin, sporting a black wig, which he quickly whipped off his head, appeared back on the stage. As another set of curtains slowly parted behind him we could see a table and chair. The scene was set.

'Hello again folks,' announced Kevin, our quizmaster. 'If you could once again put your hands together and give a round of applause for our magic maestro, The Great Whodeani. Thank you.'

Why everyone in the audience decided to do just that is a question, which can only be answered by each and every one of them, because, The *Gross* Whodeani was exactly that, gross.

'Right, ladies and gentlemen, it's quiz night at the Extra. Anyone interested in taking part will they please pop the entrance fee of two pounds each, or five-pound a couple, into the box my lovely assistant will bring to your table, and she will hand you a blank piece of paper and a pencil. Would you please put your name, or your team name, on the paper, and at the end of the quiz, she will be round again to collect them so they can be marked. Thank you everyone and good luck.'

'What type of quiz is it, then?' asked a man in the audience.

'It's a simple twenty question, general knowledge quiz with a prize of one hundred pounds for the winner, or winners,' replied the quizmaster.

'Bloody hell, a hundred quid ... that's certainly worth winning, that is,' exclaimed Alan. 'Have you got a fiver on you, Rose?'

'Yes, Alan, answered Rose, delving into her handbag. 'Here we are ... pop it in her box will you.'

'What shall we call ourselves?' I asked Mary. 'I know, we'll be known as The Bent City Danglers. What about you lot?'

'Rose and I will call ourselves The Big Fact Hunt,' replied Alan. 'Won't we, Rose.'

'Bugger, I'd thought of that one,' said Mick, sounding a bit miffed.

'I know,' giggled Chris. 'We'll call ourselves Tequila Mockingbird.'

'Why not Norfolk And Good?'

'Behave, Mick, please.'

The tension was rising. The thought of winning one hundred pounds had whetted the appetite of everyone, so much so, there were no takers for the bar. In fact, when the rumour got round, the bar quickly emptied of those who had ducked out of the magic show.

By this time, Kevin had seated himself behind the table and was shuffling through a small pile of papers. Finding what he was looking for, he brought his hand down loudly on the table-top and called for everyone's attention.

'Let the quiz begin,' he shouted at the top of his voice. Right, ladies and gentlemen, no googling, and turn all iPhones off. Question number one ... what is the most common colour of toilet paper in France?'

Mary and I knew the answer to that and quickly wrote it down - pink. We'd not long returned from a holiday in Paris, and as I looked around, I could see a lot of pencils being chewed by people looking upwards to the ceiling, hoping for divine intervention - an answer, the correct answer. A lot of whispering was going on, but thanks to the annoyance of our coach driver, and the excruciating screams of his microphone, I was now proficient in lip reading. I could detect every colour being mentioned, other than pink. Great, I thought, Mary and I could be on to a winner here.

'Question number two ... if you dug a hole through the centre of the earth starting in Wellington, New Zealand, which European Country would you end up in?'

'That's easy,' I whispered to Mary. 'It's Spain.'

'Are you sure? I reckon it could be Bicester Village in that bag shop,' replied Mary thoughtfully.

'No, it's definitely Spain.'

The quiz was going swimmingly. I had heard Alan and Rose arguing over brown toilet paper, and Mick and Chris complaining there were no questions on West Life, Chris's favourite boy band. Their answer to question number ten was completely wrong. The celebrity who picked out a picture of Mike Tyson, thinking it was a picture of himself, was not Tony Blair, but Robert Redford.

'Right, ladies and gentlemen,' shouted the quizmaster. 'If I could have your attention, please. Question number eighteen ... who invented the word vomit?'

'Blimey, I reckon we've got every question right so far,' I whispered to Mary. 'It was old Bill Shakespeare.'

'Are you sure it wasn't that Nick Park bloke. Wasn't it him, who made that stupid Wallace and Vomit cartoon thing?'

We were nearing the end of the quiz, and we were so excited. I had seen a nice pair of shoes in a shop back in Banbury, and Mary had spotted a nice handbag in the pound shop.

'The last question ladies and gentlemen. Question number twenty ... who wrote the book, *The Strange Stories Of Doctor Ulebuhle*, a youth and folk book, and in what year was it published?'

Bloody hell, we had it nailed. The strange stories of Doctor Ulebuhle was one of my favourite books. I'd bought two copies in case I wore one of them out turning the pages. I could picture the opening line in my mind's eye - *"My dear young friends, before you read the stories of Doctor Ulebuhle, you surely want to know how they came about and what the reason for the Ulebuhle is"*.

'If I could have your attention, please,' barked our quizmaster. 'Thank you to all those of you who took part, and if you could pass your answer papers to my delightful assistant so they can be marked, we will then find out who the lucky winner is. In the meantime the bar is open.'

'It's in the bag, we've got every question right,' I said proudly. 'How did you both get on?' I turned to Alan and Rose.

'I reckon we did all right,' replied Alan. 'Rose thought it was Henry the Eighth, who introduced a wife tax, and the correct name for a question mark is a round thing with a bit sticking out. That sounded about right to me.'

'What about you and Chris, Mick,' I asked turning to them . 'Any good?'

'Yes, mate, I reckon we've done well, although we got a bit stuck on the question about the unicorns. I thought a collection of unicorns was a blessing but

Chris said she was sure it was a load of white horses, with pricks on the front of their heads. We went with Chris because she knows a lot about them and those sorts of things, don't you, love?'

'Yeah, I had to laugh. Mick reckoned the boiling point of water was ninety degrees, but I said don't be so bloody stupid, ninety degrees is the boiling point of a right-angle bloody triangle .. the silly sod.'

A question mark is a round thing with a bit sticking out? A wife tax? Pricks on their heads, and right-hand bloody boiling triangles? We couldn't wait to get our hands on the money. Sadly, it was not to be. How could I have made such a basic mistake?

'I could murder that bloody freak, so I could,' I said angrily.

'Calm down Phil, it was just a simple mistake. Nobody got all the questions right. Missing a couple of dots out was no big deal,' Mary said trying to console me.

'Ere, Phil. You and Mary did get every question right, so why didn't that berk give you the hundred quid?'

'He missed a couple of dots out in one of the answers, Mick,' replied Mary.

'Which question was that, then? Was it the one where he asked for the name of the country that had one hundred and fifty-eight verses in its national anthem?'

'What ... Greece? No, it wasn't that one ... it was the last question.'

'But you and he got the right answer. I heard him

say so. I heard you both cheering. So why did he change his bloody mind and cross your answer out?'

'I missed some dots out, Mick. The bloke who wrote the book, *The Strange Stories Of Doctor Ulebuhle*, a youth and folk book, was a chap by the name of Bruno H Burgel, and it was published in 1920.'

'I know, and that's what the quizmaster said. So what was wrong with that?' queried Mick.

'Umlaut, mate,' I replied.

''Ere, Phil ... there's no need to be rude to my Mick. He only asked a question, didn't you Mick?' said Chris up in arms.

'I did, love.'

'No, you don't understand mate,' I explained. 'I missed the umlaut over the u in Burgel. It's two dots, which are written over the top of a vowel in German, to indicate a different vowel quality. It changes the sound of the letter.'

'Oh, now you've explained it, it serves you right, you silly sod. Every bugger knows how to spell that German bloke's name properly, don't we, Chris?'

'Yes, Mick. We certainly do, love.'

'We knew that as well, didn't we Rose?'

'Yes, Alan, we did.'

'Come on, Mary. Let's get out of here. I need a stiff drink.'

'We ain't paying their prices,' said Mary as we left the room.

'No worries,' I smiled. 'I smuggled a bottle in your suitcase.'

'My suitcase ... why not in yours?'

'I didn't want to get caught when Kevin searched our luggage. You know, when we first got here.'

Chapter 17

'What do you mean one pound; I gave you forty quid. What's with the one pound?' queried a refined looking gentleman, standing in front of me at the reception desk.

'It's a refund for the cancelled trip to Fantasy Island,' replied Kevin. He explained that he'd had a change of heart with regard to issuing refunds for any trips that had been cancelled due to circumstances beyond the control of the person who'd booked the trip, or himself as in this case.

I had remembered someone earlier threatening to kill him if he didn't get his money back. I think the threat of being killed may have persuaded him.

'I gave you forty friggin quid for that excursion. What are you on about, a single pound refund? You're having a laugh, ain't you. How in hell do you work that one out?' shouted the, by now, very angry gentleman.

'It's the surcharge.'

'Surcharge ... what bloody surcharge?' yelled the gentleman, extremely angry now.

'The ninety seven and a half percent surcharge. It's in the hotel rule book on page twelve. I can work it out for you, if you want me to,' replied Kevin holding his ground.

'Work it out!' spluttered the gentleman. 'What do you mean, work it out? Are you suggesting I'm bloody thick or summat?'

'No sir, not for a minute, far from it, but if I might show you,' replied Kevin. 'It appears to me your standard of education is a little, how can I put it ... rather wanting, sir.'

'You better had pal, otherwise you'll be hard pushed to make it through till dinner time.'

'Oh, good, it's really quite simple, sir. Let me explain in simple terms,' continued Kevin, taking a pad and pen from under the desk. 'We assume that the number forty is one hundred per cent because it's the output value of the task, and let us assume that x is the value we're looking for ... right? Now, if one hundred per cent equals forty, we can write it down as 100% = 40. We know that x per cent equals one of the output value, so we can write it down as x% = 1. Still following me, sir?'

'Er aye ... what? Er, yes ... yes, I'm following you. Of course I am you idiot. Do you think I'm bloody stupid?'

'No need to be facetious. Good ... now we have two simple equations,' Kevin was writing the figures down on his pad. '100% = 40 and x = 1 where the left sides of both of the equations have the same units, and the right sides also have the same units. It therefore follows that 100%/x% = 40/1. Do you not agree that it's simple?

'Er ... yes ... I suppose it is,' acknowledged the, by now puzzled, gentleman.

'Right, so we agree that $100\%/x/\% = 40/1$ ... therefore it follows that $(100/x)*x = (40/1)*x$, and what you end up with is, $100/40 = x$. From where I'm standing, $100/40 = x$, and thus $x = 2.5$. So there we are ... 2.5% of forty pounds is one pound. Easy peasy, is it not?'

'Oh ... er ... yeah, I suppose so. Hmm, I can see what you mean now. Bloody hell I'm so sorry, thank you very very much,' replied the, by now, very grateful gentleman as he walked off with a swagger and a smile on his face.

'Oh, I do like a satisfied customer. Ah, Mr and Mrs Sleet-Street. I have your refund all ready for you here.'

There was no point in arguing about the pronunciation of our surname, or going over the same mathematical argument about the one pound refund again. I just wanted to grab the pound and stick it in Kevin's eye. Taking the pound, I slipped it into my pocket, squeezing it as hard as I could without breaking a fingernail, turned and walked away and back up to our room.

'Have you paid this moron the extra money for the journey home?' my wife, Mary asked as I went through the door. 'When we get back I'm going to ring up that D*on't Get Dom Get Done*, bald-headed bloke off the telly and have a word with him.'

'What's all this about paying extra for the return journey?' I enquired. looking puzzled.

'You obviously haven't read the hotel's

information book, have you? Naughty boy ... it's all down here. Have a look,' replied Mary showing me.

If only I had got those dots in the right place.....

Chapter 18

For the genuine lovers of the countryside, as distinct from the connoisseurs of the spectacular, nature has always had a charm of its own. And this part of our country, it may be said, has a patent for a certain type of scenery, featureless and flat.

English towns and villages differ strikingly from those in other countries. There is no prim uniformity, no trees purposely planted for shade, no portioning of sunlight; beauty just occurs unplanned.

Each century has had a hand in shaping the countryside to some extent. A church was built here and a castle left there, now and again there is a ruined abbey. There are the grass covered mounds of Saxon chieftains, and a rubble of stones, which was once a camp. The gable and moated manor houses, the mossy walls that were built hundreds of years ago and are now falling apart.

Is not the English countryside the work of our poets. The spring, the wildflowers, the lark and the nightingale. Nature is forever arriving and forever departing. It is forever approaching and forever disappearing. The English countryside has a uniqueness all its own.

The romance of a seaside holiday as such, needs no prolegomenon, no preliminary introduction, but the underlying experiences of any story is an obvious purpose. There were no organised trips for today, so we decided to, once again, catch a bus into the centre of Skegness. We had all agreed there was still a lot of exploring to do.

The tallest feature we witnessed on our way, was a mound of gravel, which had been positioned in a layby by the side of the road, and left there for the purpose of dressing the worn-out surface. I thanked God that we had been fortunate in choosing the right time of year to visit the area. Had it been the height of summer, no doubt we would have found ourselves stuck in an endless queue of traffic.

Councils never seem to do these necessary jobs when the roads are free of tourists. There must be a sadist in every council office throughout the country, planning on how he might ruin and shorten a holiday-makers seaside trip by at least two days, by carrying out his evil intent. They must have Barbi and Ken fashionista dolls in their offices. Ken dressed in his trunks with his surfboard, and Barbi with her swim and dive accessories, and they most likely have them jammed into a camper van, ready to start sticking pins into them as soon as the sun shines.

The bus stopped and we alighted at what had become our usual dropping off point, on the oddly named Scarborough Esplanade, close to a Macdonald's takeaway.

'I'm starving,' announced Alan.

'You can't be, you've just eaten a whole load of those Chia seed things for breakfast.'

'I only had two bloody teaspoonfuls; I thought we were the first guests into the dining room this morning, but we evidently weren't. Some gutsy bugger must have got there before us and nicked the four weetabix. When I asked that Kevin idiot why he hadn't put more food out he said he didn't like it when food was wasted. *"Have some bite-sized shreddies instead,"* he said to me, but there was only one bugger left in the bowl.'

'What did he say to that, then?' enquired Mick.

'The cheeky bugger told me to get up earlier instead of lying in bed. Lying in bed, I said ... I was down here at five o'clock on the dot.'

'And what did Kevin say to that?'

'Told me they'd stopped serving at four thirty. Said he could get me some pumpkin seeds but guess what, there would be an extra charge.'

I remember thinking that Alan might possibly be whistling like a budgie when the time came for us to return home.

He was not the only one suffering from malnutrition, we all were. Chris had started out on our holiday as a next to nothing and now she was stick thin and dragging her feet. Likewise Rose; her jaw had started to head south, because she barely had the strength to keep it from dropping onto the top of her boobs. Mary was even worse; she was getting heavier on my arm, because of her need for extra support.

Our first port of call was the snack bar in Funland,

an amusement arcade directly opposite the pleasure beach, on the Scarborough Esplanade. The waitress who came to our table must have been a first responder, because she looked alarmingly at us, and appeared quite concerned. We refused her offer of intravenous drips and a multi-vitamin supplement and settled for six cups of tea and a few rounds of toast with jam.

'I would get some sugar into yourselves,' she said to us sagely. 'If you faint and fall over, I'll have to get the boss to drag you out to the pavement; there's that many forms to fill in. We could get a bad reputation, you know ... people might think it's our bacon rolls.' She pleaded with us to remain upright at least until we had finished eating and stepped outside.

After our sugar rush, we walked a little further along the front until we reached the Meanie BoBini's bar, grill and friary. Alan, Rose and Chris were exhausted, as was Mary. The jam had yet to take its effect and provide us with a much needed energy boost.

How often is it that we men hear our wives exclaim, *"What shall we have to eat?"* and immediately follow the question with a raft of choices and not one of those choices includes the words, *"Anything will do"*. However, they were the exact words used by our womenfolk when they were asked by a waitress who attended our table, as to what they would like to eat.

'Anything will do,' they said in unison, much to the surprise of the waitress.

After a very satisfying feast, we ambled further

along the front with renewed vigour taking in all the sights and sounds of this busy seaside town. Wandering into The Jolly Fisherman for a drink, we had forgotten what it was like to pay for one outside the confines of our hotel, and as a result Mary and myself, and Alan and Rose queried the price of the round, which Mick and Chris treated us to.

'Bloody hell, I'd forgotten how cheap a pint of beer is,' said Alan with astonishment.

As we left the pub, we had more spring in our step than the cast of *Strictly Come Dancing*, and holidaymakers began to clap and shout *"bravo"*. I heard someone shouting, *"it must be them off the telly"*.

We stopped for a while to gaze over the fence at the Jolly Roger's adventure golf. It brought back painful memories for Alan, who told us that the only two decent balls he had ever hit in his entire golfing career, were when he trod on the head of a rake in a sand bunker. My own memory was of forgetting who I had been partnered with, and when I fired the ball off the tee, I did not see my partner again until I was putting on the eighteenth green, and then I wasn't able to recognise him. My balls could fly anywhere, which they often did.

We knew it was getting near the end of all the excitement, the word *Bar* had been dropped in preference to *Restaurant*. It was time to retrace our steps, and get back to the hotel so we could search for the Loss Vagas Hotel Extra's library.

I was walking towards reception to enquire of the idiot behind it, where I might find a book to read when my attention was suddenly caught by something I heard a lady saying to her husband.

'I'm looking forward to this Clairvoyant.'

Clairvoyant - had I heard the lady right?

'Excuse me,' I interrupted. 'Did I just hear you say something about a Clairvoyant?'

'Yes, that's right. There's a notice on the information board ... a woman called Mastic Meg. I'm sure I've heard her name before, I reckon she's been on the telly. I'm so excited ... I would love to hear my Winker bark one more time.'

'Winker,' I queried. 'Who is Winker then?'

'He was my little Shizhu. We lost him a while back, you know. Ted reversed the car over him on our drive.'

'Was the poor little creature deaf or something, then?'

'No, it wasn't my little Shizhu who was deaf, it was my Ted. He couldn't hear poor little Winker yelping as his insides were being squeezed out. A right bloody mess it was ... took months for the rain to wash it all away, didn't it Ted.'

A Clairvoyant - now this sounded interesting. I wonder whether, or not, Mastic Meg, or whatever her name was supposed to be, would be able to tell Alan how he could beat the gutsy bugger to the weetabix bowl in the morning.....

Chapter 19

A sceptical person is one who believes the evidence of his senses, a person who has a lot to say about both common and horse sense. Clairvoyance is thought to be an extra sense similar to that of intuition, and appears to the extrasensory perception of reality. An ability to acquire supernatural knowledge of facts and happenings in the distance, or in the past and future, independent of the ordinary senses and of the telepathic reading of the thoughts of others.

Crystal gazing is another method of getting in touch with what is called the astral plane. A crystal ball serves to focus the psychic energy of the person, in such a way that the astral senses are made to function more easily than usual. However, a believer must be cautioned against considering the crystal ball, or magic mirror, as possessing a particular magic power in itself. Rather, they simply serve as a physical instrument for astral vision, just as the telescope or microscope performs a similar function for physical vision.

A clairvoyant is someone, usually a woman, who has the power of seeing with the help of a crystal ball, things that are invisible to their audience, namely that they are a load of gullible idiots stupid enough to go along with the rubbish which spills out.

I think this was the first time on the holiday that the entertainment area was packed to the gunnels. Those attending the show were asked to pen a question to Mastic Meg and place it in a dish, which was on top of a stool, covered with a purple cloth, and positioned next to, and in front of, the stage.

How this woman got to be sitting on the stage I had no idea. One minute the stage was empty, but in the next instant there she was, sitting there in some sort of purple and black cloak, decorated with silver shapes of the moon and stars.

The laughing started, when after raising her hands above her head, she asked the audience if anybody was out there, and everyone responded with a yes. It got worse when a little voice at the back of the room shouted, is there a Winker here.

'Yes, he's over here, and I'm married to him,' shouted a woman's voice from the darkness.

'Me too,' shouted another, which then set off a barage of *me toos* around the room.

There followed an hour of complete stupidity, which began when Mastic Meg took the little sheets of paper, on which questions had been written, out of the dish she had now placed by her side, and began reading them out. Everyone, bar two audience members - one of whom wanted to know who you had to shag to get out of this hell hole, and the other if there was an escape tunnel where it could be found - wanted six numbers for Saturday night's Lotto draw.

'That's a bloody stupid question, that is,' said Chris. 'If we all win, then it won't be worth it at all?'

'Yeah, it'll be worth bugger all,' agreed Mick.

Alan and Rose were both disappointed as they thought they might have been on to a winner when they shouted. 'What's for breakfast tomorrow morning.'

Everyone else in the audience then followed by shouting the same question, apart from one chap who said in a loud voice that they couldn't survive on only four bloody weetabix. Alan wasn't quick enough to see who it was before Mastic Meg responded with the same as yesterday.

'Where is he,' demanded Alan loudly. 'Where's the greedy bugger who nicked all the bloody weetabix?'

Sorry mate, it looks as though you'll be having Chia seeds once again, I thought to myself.

Mastic Meg told us the brain is an organ with which we think what we think. It is so highly honoured that it is compensated by exemption from the duty of rational thought. It was at this point that a woman somewhere in the audience shouted,

'My old man's brains are in his bloody trousers.'

Despite the ribaldry, Mastic Meg eventually managed to get the attention of everyone in the audience, but it was turning into a bit of a circus where the animals, in this case Meg, was watching the audience acting like bloody fools.

Unfortunately, she managed to get her last prediction wrong when, on the stroke of ten o'clock, she stood up and said g*ood night everyone*, to which everyone shouted back, *no*. She quickly disappeared through the curtains.

All of a sudden the sound of a God Almighty crash came from the back of the stage behind the curtains.

'Are you alright Kev,' Mrs Hiscock shouted. 'I told you not to wear that bleeding cloak.'

'Bloody hell, my head hurts,' Kevin moaned back. 'I couldn't see that friggin thing in the bloody dark.'

'Didn't see a friggin thing?' queried Mary looking confused. 'I thought she was supposed to be a clairvoyant.'

I do not normally drink the stuff but as it was Mick's turn at the bar, I felt the need to share a single part thunder-and-lightning, one part remorse, three parts bloody murder, and five parts clarified Satan, in other words to partake in a brandy.

'Would you like anything in it, Phil,' asked Mick

'Yes mate, a slice of lemon please ... that is, if there isn't an extra charge!'

Chapter 20

Many of the hotels that Mary and I have stayed in, in the past, have had a small library. A selection of books, which guests can borrow to read in a quiet moment.

Most, if not all people, like a story. Many can recall a book they read when they were children - stories that inspired, entertained or educated.

It might be raining outside, but with a good book there is an opportunity to escape into a quiet room, away from the hustle and bustle of the everyday life in a busy hotel, and its noisy guests. There may be books you have never heard of or seen before; writers you may have heard of but never found the time or opportunity to investigate their work. There may even be a book you have heard of but unable to get a copy.

After breakfast, Mary and I then decided to go and investigate...

'I've read that ... bloody years ago. I ask you, *Noddy Goes to Toyland* ... that's a kids book. The hotel doesn't accept kids, it says adults only on the blurb, which is why I booked this particular hotel in the first place.'

Mary and I had been beaten to it. A man and a

woman, fellow travellers who hailed from Winchester, were slumped in, what looked like very uncomfortable, armchairs. The man was leaning forward, sorting through a collection of books, which were jammed into a small bookcase in the corner of the lounge. Piled on top was a collection of periodicals, two of which, Hello and OK magazines, at least offered Mary a chance to discover who had got snared and who got ditched in the world of fashion and celebrity.

'That's bloody years old, that is,' said the man. 'Look, even the M1 isn't shown in it. What use is that, for God's sake? And what's this, *The Scrummy Ponies Hacking Handbook* ... Jesus.'

'Ooh, I like the sound of that one,' replied his wife. 'Can I have a look, please? Here you take this one, you might find it a lot more interesting.'

'*Cooking On A Ration*,' chortled the woman's husband. '*One Thousand And One Ways To Cook With Tripe*? Bloody hell what a load of tripe this is.'

The man was perfectly correct, of course, not just a load of tripe, but a complete load of tripe.

Eventually, the man and his wife hauled themselves out of the uncomfortable looking armchairs and walked out the lounge. The woman was looking about furtively, and when she caught Mary's eye, offered the faintest of embarrassing smiles. She had secreted a magazine, which she'd rolled up and pushed into the rather large handbag she was holding.

When they'd finally disappeared, I picked up a

book, which according to a sticky label affixed to the front cover, proudly proclaimed it to be, The latest addition to our extensive library - *A Comprehensive Guide To The European Polecat's Saliva And Scent Glands*. Looks interesting, I thought to myself; perhaps I'll give it a go. I was just getting to the more interesting parts of the narrative when my attention was drawn to the sound of Chris's voice and an argument, which appeared to be taking place in the reception area. Although the book was extremely interesting, particularly the section relating to the anal scent glands, I felt an urgent need to investigate what the shouting was all about. It turned out to be an argument over a toilet roll, which had not been delivered to Mick and Chris's room as promised.

'My husband, Mick, is having to use the bloody curtain,' Chris was shouting at the person on reception, and whereby at this point, the woman standing behind in the queue felt the need to join in the argument.

'A toilet roll ... my you're lucky love, you are,' she said in a loud voice. 'I've been using one of our pillowcases since we got here. My husband hasn't got a clean corner left on his handkerchief, and he's already thrown away a good pair of socks.'

'Ooh pillowcases, that's a bit posh,' replied Chris, turning round to face the woman, while folding her arms across her chest and lifting her chin as far it would go.

'We always pay extra to make our holidays that bit more comfortable, love,' the woman flung back, crossing her arms over her much larger chest and lifting her chin even higher.

Oh dear, I thought it was probably not the best time to get involved and raise the issues we also had with our room. The suspicious-looking patches on the fitted sheet on our bed; was it tea, or was it not to be tea, that would be the question? It could wait for another time, and besides, I found the European polecat's anal scent glands a lot more interesting, and a much better read than the Scrummy Ponies Hacking Handbook.

Sadly, I was forced to give up on, *The Comprehensive Guide To The European Polecat's Saliva And Scent Glands*, after I discovered that quite a lot of pages were missing, and someone had written - good toilet paper - on one of the remaining pages. Suddenly it clicked, and I realised why so many of the other books had missing pages. Why, *The Gangster's Guide To Making Money In Your Spare Time*, consisted of only the first and last pages, and *The Little Book Of Toilet Humour*, had no pages at all. So where had the M1 gone? There was only one book I found, which had not been vandalised, a book entitled, *Help With Visual Latin Translation*. Why this had not been damaged was anyone's guess, most likely because someone had written the word - fascinating - at the very top of an inside page.

I just had to have a quick read and I'm glad I did because it proved to be revelatory. I hadn't realised the big difference between English and Latin prose, is that while modern English is largely a language of short, separate sentences, Latin expresses the sense of the passage as a whole, and keeps the climax in abeyance until the delivery of the very last word. Wow, I thought, you learn something new every day. I was hooked, but out of the blue my concentration was interrupted.

'Ere Phil, you like tits, don't you?' Mary suddenly asked me.

I was quite taken aback. *"I like tits"* was a question I had never thought I'd hear my darling wife ask me. What a gem. I certainly do have an interest in tits - in fact, I love them, but as it turned out, not the *Thorburn's Book of Birds* type. In my naivety, I had visualised a saucy, top of the shelf magazine.

I was just about to leave the lounge with the interesting book on Latin translation under my arm, which I thought I might read, later in my room, when the hotel owner stopped me. He drew my attention to a security camera and a notice affixed to the entrance door into the lounge, which said, *"There is an extra charge for the reading of all library books"*. Bloody hell, Mary and I had been caught on camera, and God only knows how much of a bill we had clocked up without realising. Incidentally, what does the word bollocks translate to in Latin? I thought I would never be able to find out.

'It's the same in Latin as it is in English,' Alan answered, interrupting my thoughts.

'Really?'

The word bollocks did reappear when I recounted my experience with the Latin translation book, and how Mary and I had both been caught on camera. We were later to discover that there were security cameras all over the hotel, and it suddenly dawned on me about a comment I had overheard when I was standing in a short queue at reception. The man at the front had told his wife to smile and say *cheese* when she picked up one of the hotel's biros, which had been set aside for the use of the guests - for an extra charge, of course.

'Yes, my mate, Dave Russell, told me the word was first used by Julius Caesar.'

'What did this Russell mate of yours say about it, then ... that is by way of an explanation for it being used?' I enquired.

'He said that when the old lemon squeezer himself, stepped from his boat at Dover all those years ago, he asked a local where he was, and when this bloke told him, the Caesar chap said, *"But I can't be"*.'

'Now why did he say that? Didn't he think he was in the right place, then?'

'No, it wasn't that. He thought he had landed in bloody Eygpt. One of his generals told him he'd had his map upside down.'

I looked across at Mick and Chris, and they were looking just as surprised as I was, to hear this gem of information.

'Blimey, you learn something new every day, don't you, Chris,' said Mick in amazement.

Chapter 21

It was an early start and the sun had not yet fully risen, but already there was lots of colour in the eastern sky. Outside our window, there was a large tree with a cloud of thin foliage floating high in the summer air. I heard a thrush singing, filling the decorative, early glow of sunlight with a golden sound.

An open-air market conjured up thoughts of stalls filled with produce. Men in coats carrying marbled note books. A mountain range of potatoes rising up behind hills of cabbages, strings of onions suspended from rails and bundles of purple grapes, as well as crates of tangerines, and pears and figs nestling in soft tissue-lined heavy duty cardboard boxes.

I thought we would make our way around the stalls until we could find the flowers, where, undoubtedly, there would be a crowd of both young, and matronly ladies, milling around a mass of blooms. There would be satisfying solidarity in the glorious abundance of smells, and a picture of a harem sprung into my mind. African violets, solid spots of blue, providing a contrast to a majestic display of roses, and a dewy forest of maidenhair ferns.

With the penetrating aroma of green fruits permeating the heavy scent of flowers, I could just picture the farms in far off lands, the fruit pickers with straw hats covering their faces, and in the distance the mountains rising behind a motionless blue sea. There is nothing like a smell to stir the memory.

It was the last full day of our holiday as the following day we would be travelling back to our respective homes. Mick and Chris would be the first in our little group, lucky enough to escape the torture and make a run for it. Alan and Rose, and Mary and I would have to wait that little bit longer to gain our freedom.

'I'll kill that bastard, I will,' muttered a man, with a socially irresponsible and unacceptable comb-over, as he climbed onto the coach. 'If I hear any more excuses, he's dead.'

I think he hailed from somewhere near Southampton, and what that was all about, I had no idea. Whatever it was, it sounded pretty serious.

The itinerary for today was a drive along, what Kevin said was a stunning coastline, with panoramic views of lakes and mountains, of mighty rivers and spectacular waterfalls, bettered only by those to be seen on the mighty Congo River.

'Where are we going, then?' shouted a woman at the back of the coach. 'Forget all that scenery bollocks, we want to go shopping, don't we girls? We want to buy handbags.'

There were shouts of approval from all the other women.

'Yeah, let's hit the old man's wallet hard,' another shouted.

'Yeah, and when we get back, we'll be ready for the stripper,' another woman said with a dirty laugh.

I looked across at Alan and Mick

'Stripper, I know nothing about any stripper,' Alan said, raising his eyebrows. 'I'm up for some of that, mate, I can tell you. A bit of pole dancing ... bring it on.'

'You won't be, mate when I tell you the stripper's a bloke,' said Mick putting Alan right.

'What one of them Chippendale freaks?'

No, *The Bodger,* the stripping specialist. Kevin told me he always keeps his hat on.'

God Almighty, please God, no. Just when I thought things were getting more civilised, a stripping Bodger had been thrown into the mix.

'Sorry darlings, we're off to Mablethorpe first,' shouted back Kevin.

'Mablethorpe? I've heard of that. Have they got mountains and a waterfall there as well, then?' enquired Rose.

'I don't think so ... in fact, I know so. They haven't got either I'm afraid,' I answered. 'It's just another one of Kevin's sick jokes.'

It is the frequency and quality of English pubs, which makes it appealingly possible to discover England as it is best seen. Ours is not a country with segregated wonders separated by long stretches of road. With every mile, there is something to be admired and you cannot fail to observe the surprising variety of natural scenery packed into so small a place.

There is the ruggedness and bucolic softness of Devon and Cornwall. The gentle emptiness of the South Downs with their chalky contours. The romantic woodlands and hilly pastures of the Midland Counties, and the wistfulness of the Lincolnshire fens. Unfortunately, regarding the country pubs, we passed many but did not stop, that is, until we reached Mablethorpe where an opportunity presented itself.

The coach came to a grinding halt in the High Street, at the corner where the Quebec and Gibraltar roads meet, opposite a concreted walkway entrance to the beach.

'Right everyone, I am not allowed to stop here for too long, so if you can exit the coach as quickly as possible, please. Remember to be back on the coach by four o'clock, so we will get back in time for your final evening meal, which a little birdie has told me, will be something special.'

Oh no, I thought, surely not a Baked Alaska; the hotel will go up in smoke and take us all with it.

'Don't forget ladies and gentlemen,' continued Kevin. 'Tonight will be the big night. The Bodger will be coming to do a special performance, but I must point out to those of you with a weak stomach, it will get more than a little dirty at the end ... so be prepared. Thank you, and enjoy your afternoon here in Mablethorpe. Be sure to look out for the open-air market on the edge of town.'

I found it an unexpectedly weird experience walking through Mablethorpe, after spending the last few days exploring Skegness, where I had begun to admire the plastic cosmopolitanism. There was a certain sameness here, but with some subtle differences. A multi-discount megastore boasted thousands of weekly clearance items. The Spanish City housed a market and a Kids Adventure World, and there was the Mirage and City of God, whatever they were all about. We had not seen the words *mega* or *clearance* anywhere in Skegness, nor was there any of the cockney slang - the speech of one who talks with his tongue, thinks with his lugholes, and feels the pride of a creator in accomplishing the feat of a budgerigar. No, it all looked and felt quite sophisticated.

It was not long before we realised that we needed to get back to our drop-off point, where the coach would pick us up. Our time in Mablethorpe had passed rather quickly.

'We never found that open-air market, did we?' said someone waiting in the queue for the coach. 'We walked for bloody miles, and couldn't find it anywhere.'

We hadn't been able to find it either. We had stopped and asked a man and his wife in the street for directions, but they told us they had never heard of it. The man went on to say that his greatgrandmother had been stopped in the street and asked the very same question over a hundred years earlier by none other than the renowned historical English poet Alfred, Lord Tennyson who had told her he was visiting the town. Apparently, it turned out he wanted to buy his missus something frilly, a negligible the man told us. I think he meant negligee.

'Ere, we only paid to come on this trip because my wife wanted to get a new handbag off the market. I could murder that Kevin, I could,' voiced an irate fellow traveller. 'The tosser told us it was on the edge of town, but he never said which edge ... the idiot.'

Chapter 22

The atmosphere was electric; it had been building up all afternoon. *The Las Vagas Hotel Extra* had never sold so many snowballs and schooners of sherry. Kevin had quickly run out of quavers, wotsits and cheese and onion crisps, and was down to his last few packets of smoky bacon and salt and vinegar.

'Break open the space raiders and doritos Mrs H, will you please,' he shouted from behind the bar. 'They've gone up to two quid a packet. Have we got plenty of tissues and wet wipes?'

'It will have to be a brave bloke, who wants to take a seat within an arm grabbing distance of all of those women sitting in the front row,' chortled Mick. 'My Chris is in there somewhere.'

'So is Rose,' replied Alan. 'I can hear her, but I can't see her.'

Mary had also managed to sneak in there somewhere, but like Chris and Rose, she was nowhere to be seen.

'They're like a pack of bloody savages, they are. Look at them all screaming their bloody heads off. This stripper bloke hasn't shown so much as a leg yet and they're going ballistic,' I said.

'I hope he's got a couple of minders, because he's going to need them,' said Mick, looking around the place.

It wasn't long before it started, and as the lights began to dim most, if not all, of the women began to chant - *"Bodger, Bodger, Bodger"*. It was unceasing. Hot dog rolls and slices of bread were flying through the air.

'Come on big boy, get 'em off,' one woman right at the front shouted.

''Ere, that wasn't my Chris, was it? queried Mick. 'It sounded a lot like her.'

It was now pitch black and then a spotlight flickered and flashed into action. One of the black curtains was pushed apart, and Kevin Hiscock walked onto the stage to a tumultuous round of screams and boos.

'Get him off, get him off. We want Bodger, we want Bodger, we want Bodger,' the women were chanting and clapping.

Raising his hands in the air with a plea for the audience to calm down had no effect whatsoever; he was wasting his time, so he did what the front row of the audience suggested, and walked off the stage. Then the whistling started, along with wild clapping, which quickly reverted to a slow handclap.

The curtains suddenly began to very slowly draw apart revealing four doors. A red one, white one, blue one and a green one. A few of the women were singing - *There's An Old Piano And He's Playing It Hot Behind The Green Door*. It was a terrifying sight to behold; everything was at fever pitch.

Suddenly, the green door inched open and a hand, holding a cloth cap, slowly emerged. All was bedlam.

'Thank God I put an extra pad on,' shouted a little old lady. 'Otherwise, I'd be in a right mess.'

'Grab me some tissues when you go to the bar, will you?' asked another woman in the front row.

'Grab me some too,' shouted someone else.

'You can keep your hat on ... you can keep your hat on ... you can keep your bleedin hat on,' shouted the women at the top of their voices. 'We want Bodger ... we want Bodger.' On and on it went.

I looked for Kevin and saw he had made it to the relative safety of the bar.

'You deliver the drinks, Mrs H. If I go out there, they'll tear me apart. And check that test date on the defibrillator's sticker ... we might need to use it. If the battery's flat, we're right buggered.'

It was quite concerning. Kevin and his moustachioed wife were looking terrified.

'I told you not to book him,' Mrs H screamed at her husband. 'I knew there'd be trouble. What about the Fire Safety Certificate, is that up to date? Get him on quick and let's get it over with.'

There was a drum roll and then the lights began to flash. The green door was flung open, and the cheering, clapping and screaming suddenly stopped. A little old man in a cow gown and wearing a cloth cap walked onto the stage and stood in the centre.

'Aye-up, good evening all, Reg Entwistle's t'name. I hope thee dunt mind if I kep me at on. I have bin asked t'come along toneet ant give thee all a lesson in how t'strip the paint off all these dowers with the minimum amount of fuss ... and in the minimum amount of time. What thee hast do fust is...'

After a stunned silence there was an almighty uproar. I could hear the sound of breaking glass and crisp packets were flying all over the place. Uneaten glace cherries stuck on the ends of cocktail sticks were being flicked - some quite expertly I have to say - at Fred Entwistle, and quickly dropping his cap, he beat a hasty retreat from the stage, slamming the green door shut behind him.

Women rushed forward clawing at Fred's cap, like trophy hunters, who having made a kill, wanted a part of their victim to hang on a wall or above a fireplace; perhaps even to wear. There was scratching and biting; it was a terrible sight. Babycham and sherry was everywhere, flooding the floor.

Many members of the gentler sex were baying for someone's blood, and their attention was suddenly directed to the person who had arranged this horror show. They charged en-masse, like a herd of bull elephants, towards the bar, and like the coward he was, the subject of their ire, Kevin had already disappeared.

Outside an engine could be heard starting up, but when the herd finally managed to get out the door into the pitch black of the car park, it was only to see the disappearing tail lights of a coach.

Chapter 23

It was an early start this morning. At last we were going home - yippee.

We - sorry I - had packed our holdall and suitcase the night before. We could not wait to get out of this apology for a hotel as soon as possible. Normally the guests would be asked to place their suitcases outside the bedroom door by seven in the morning, ready for a member of staff to collect them up and take them down to reception so they could be loaded onto the waiting coach.

We had declined the offer for this service after we'd discovered there would be an extra charge of five pounds for each item, including carrier bags. Therefore, it came as no surprise that as Mary and I made our way downstairs to the reception area there were forty-seven other people in front of us all trying to negotiate the stairs as the lift was still out of order. On finally reaching the ground floor we were greeted with a sight, which looked more like a war zone than a hotel reception. This area had suddenly been transformed into something that resembled a casualty clearing station.

A woman was attending to a cut over her

husband's eye. Another husband was supporting his wife's leg, while at the same time shouting for a bag of frozen peas to use as a cold compress on her twisted ankle.

'I'm dying,' someone else was yelling. 'Help me, please.'

There were casualties everywhere. The stair carpet had obviously lived up to its reputation of being a deathtrap.

Chris and Rose were standing together and staring at the floor carpet. They were undecided as to the identity of a large red mark.

'I reckon its blood,' I heard Rose say.

'I think it could be that red bean curry I saw a woman bringing up last night,' said Chris.

Whatever it was, it didn't look at all nice.

The injured were being transferred to the lounge area, where they were either seated on chairs or just laid on the dirty floor. I noticed one man, who was lying on the floor, had his bandaged ankle resting on the book I'd been reading only a few hours before - *The Comprehensive Guide To The European Polecat's Saliva And Scent Glands*.

'Where's Kevin, where in the hell is that hotel manager,' shouted the man with the socially unacceptable comb-over. 'I need to have a word with him.'

We all needed a word. We had all come here to *The Loss Vagas Hotel Extra* for a relaxing holiday, and now, one week later, just as we were about to leave, many of the group were crippled. It wasn't just the crippling results of staying in Mr Kevin Hiscock's hotel that we wanted answers to; it was an explanation for the sheet of paper, which had been pushed under all the bedroom doors in the dead of night, while we were fast asleep in the land of nod. They were the bills for all the extras we supposedly had.

'Twenty quid ... twenty friggin quid. What the hell for?' shouted an extremely angry gentleman, the refined voice I recognised as belonging to the man who had given Kevin a lesson in style, when the wearing of socks with sandals had been discussed.

'What's this for ... the use of a bottle opener?' shouted another. 'Good God, how the hell was I supposed to open a bottle of beer sold to me over the bloody bar.'

Everything was in chaos, and Kevin was nowhere to be seen. His still mustachioed wife, Mrs Hiscock, told me she had been hunting high and low for him.

'Perhaps he's gone into Skeggie for some more toilet rolls,' she said, trying to explain his absence.

'Move that friggin ambulance, will you. I need to be able to get my coach out,' shouted our friendly driver. 'I've got a job to do here, and I'm on a school run this afternoon. Come on everyone, let's be having you. We've got a long journey ahead of us, so get your cases out and stick them by the side of the coach and I'll do the rest ... thank you.'

'A pound for butter, a knob of bleedin butter. I just cannot believe it. He wants throttling. His mum and dad went to all that effort, and I bet they're so proud of him ... congratulations Miss, it's a chiselling little bastard!' exclaimed Mary angrily. 'It's a pity they never married.'

I decided to settle the bill for all our supposed extras I had no recollection of having or ordering. We had all been warned about having to pay for the return journey home; we could account for that cost. A threat to call the local constabulary persuaded me, it was probably better to pay up and wait until we made it home safely, before contacting Trading Standards and Rip-Off Britain.

Why does one of those fiddling little bars of soap, expertly wrapped in a miniscule piece of paper, cost so much, and the tiny plastic bottles of shower gel and bath foam. Every other hotel Mary and I stayed in, they were given free, as part of the cost of the room.

We had not realised the hotel had an indoor swimming pool. It did not matter apparently, we were still charged for its use even though neither Mary or myself had used it. The mustachioed monster behind the reception desk told us it was not the hotel's fault we hadn't used it, and likewise the spa centre with a range of beauty treatments.

I remembered guessing that the behemoth, who passed for Kevin's wife, was not a regular visitor. Later on I learnt that Mick and Chris had donned their swimming costumes and gone in search of the pool.

'When we got there the doors were locked, and there was a sign pinned up saying it was closed in the interests of public safety,' Mick informed us. 'There was some horrible green slime floating on the top.'

'I wanted to have a chin wax as I've got a few whiskers, and one of them is over an inch long, isn't it Mick? I couldn't find the bloody place,' said Chris.

We all paid up; it was a small price for our freedom, and there was no point in prolonging the torture any further.

I remembered little of the journey home, three unscheduled toilet breaks, the four hour stop for another repair to the coach - a new tyre by all accounts. I was dead to the world.

The only thing I do recall was being jabbed in the ribs by a fellow passenger, who was passing a hat around everyone on the coach, wanting me to put a tip for the driver in it.

His hat is probably still sitting there on the grass verge by the side of the M42....

Chapter 24

I woke with a fright and sat up in bed stunned, rubbing my eyes as a sudden flood of light greeted me as Mary threw back the bedroom curtains and opened the window.

'Who the hell is it?' she shouted, leaning out and looking down towards the ground.

My dream was broken, the jackpot lottery win was nothing more than just that - a dream. The strong contrasting features of the scene before me began to etch into my consciousness, as I found myself experiencing something of split personality feeling. I seemed to be living two lives at once, but in two separate places, with two separate sets of incidents going on. Anthea Turner had suddenly snatched the cheque for two million pounds from me, and now I seemed to be divided between two irreconcilable streams of thought; the Ferrari or the magnificent house with its elaborate furnishings, and glimpses of St Tropez, with crowds of impatient people huddled around me as I surfaced into reality.

'What the hell is going on?' I managed to squeak, still half asleep.

'There's a copper at the front door. What in hell

have you been up to?' asked my long suffering wife, Mary.

'Nothing,' I replied. 'I've done nothing wrong. I only ride my bike in the daytime now, since I was booked for having a duff battery in its rear light. Ere, he could be here to see you, you know?'

'What do you mean ... me? Are you accusing me of something? I've done bugger all wrong ... well, not as far as I can remember. Go and see what he wants, Phil. I've got next to nowt on ... my nightie wasn't dry enough to wear last night. You forgot to bring it in from the line before it started raining.'

I crept downstairs to the front door and after releasing the safety chain opened it up, where I was confronted by a copper as tall as the spire on St Michael's Church in Coventry.

'Am I speaking to Mr Sleet-Street?' he enquired.

I told him that my name was, in fact, Street, not Sleet-Street and yes, I was probably the person he wanted to speak to.

'May I come in then please Mr Sleet-Street-Street?' he respectfully asked pulling his helmet off.

I directed him to the lounge and shouted up the stairs to Mary, asking her to come down and put the kettle on and make us all a cup of tea.

Police Officer Dixon sat down on the most comfortable of our most uncomfortable armchairs and pulled a small notebook from the top pocket of his tunic.

'I am here to ask you a few questions about a recent holiday you've been on. I belive it was a visit to

The Loss Vagas Hotel Extra in Skegness, is that correct?' enquired PC Dixon.

'Oh dear,' replied Mary. 'I knew I shouldn't have done it. I'm so terribly sorry, officer, I don't know what went through my bleedin head. I'll go and get it now.'

'Er ... what are you talking about? What have you been up to, then?' I queried.

'I won't be a mo. I've got it right here.'

'I haven't come here to take back the ashtray you nicked, Mrs Sleet-Street-Street. Although now you come to mention it, I will need to take a note of what you have just admitted doing,' said PC Dixon, licking the lead in his pencil and noting the word *thief* in his notebook; spelling it out as he wrote it down.

'Thief has got an *i* in it, constable,' I said correcting him.

'Er, yes ... thank you. The reason I have come here is on a much more important matter. It concerns the disappearance of a man, who goes by the name of Mr Kevin Hiscock.'

'Jesus, has he disappeared, then?' enquired Mary. 'The big knob ... has he run off? I wouldn't be at all surprised; you should see the look of that wife of his. She needed some work doing, I can tell you. Got a face like a bag of bloody spanners and a body that looks like a relief map of the bloody Himalayas. My husband said her tits looked like a dead heat in a hot air balloon race. Hot air balloons, I ask you? They looked more lop-sided to me. An ugly cow that one, definitely gone to seed.'

Harmony among women has always proved to be problematic. It is merely a postponement of malice. However, what is not forgotten is that part of a skull into which they intend to bury a hatchet.

'Ere, Mary, how do you know he's got a big knob?' I asked, raising my eyebrows.

'Sorry sir, madam ... if I may interrupt. I have been asked to escort you both back to the main police station in Skegness to answer some further questions regarding the disappearance of Mr Hiscock. If this noddy car they've given me doesn't break down, we should be there sometime after lunch.'

'Oh, shall I make a few sandwiches then? Will cheese and pickle be all right?' Mary enquired of the constable.

Fortunately PC Dixon's car stood the test and we arrived back in Skegness at the time he had predicted. We walked together into the police station and what followed could only be described as a lightning strike, a bolt out of the blue. Standing there before us, and lining a very long corridor were the other forty seven holidaymakers, who had been on our coach and stayed at the same hotel. I instantly recognised Alan and Rose, and Mick and Chris.

'Hello again girls,' said Mary to Rose and Chris. 'What brings you here? Would any of you like a cheese and pickle sarnie ... I made far too many, and they're rather filling. See you later.'

There wasn't a happy face amongst them; not a smile or nod of recognition from anybody. Everyone had a terrified look on their face, everywhere there was silence, a silence broken only when someone shouted *"next"* from a room at the far end of the corridor. PC Dixon, the officer who had escorted us to the station tapped me on the shoulder.

'Mr Sleet-Street-Street, please come this way.'

I walked the entire length of the corridor, and at one stage when I looked back, I noticed Mary sitting on a chair and wiping her eyes with my white handkerchief - she had obviously found a clean corner. She was talking to Rose and Chris, and they appeared to be consoling one another. When we reached the end door, PC Dixon knocked on it gently. Suddenly a booming voice from inside the room shouted *"enter"*.

'Ah, Mr Sleet-Street-Street, come in and take a seat, please. This is Detective Sergeant Plank and I am Detective Constable Kennelly. Thank you, Dixon, that will be all.'

I did as invited, sitting down at a small table opposite two officers, whom I assumed were members of the local constabulary. However, it turned out they were, in actual fact, members of an elite branch of specially trained CID officers connected to Scotland Yard in London, and who had been drafted in by the local constabulary to help solve, what was for them, a baffling case.

'Right Kennelly, how the bloody hell do you get this tape machine thing working?' barked DS Plank.

'It's just there, Sarge ... the little red button,' replied DC Kennelly. 'Just press it down and it should start recording.'

'What, this one?'

'No, Sarge, the one next to it. You've just gone and ejected the tape.'

'Oh yes, so I have. It's this one then, you say?'

'No, no, no. Now you've gone and turned the machine off,' said Kennelly in exasperation.

'Bleeding thing, these fiddling knobs are far too bloody small and complicated for me. What's that you just said?'

'I said it was a nice day outside, Sarge. Mr Sleet-Street-Street just coughed.'

I was getting a little concerned. I had the feeling that Sergeant Plink, Plank, Plonk, or whatever his bloody name was, was more than just a little hard of hearing.

'This is going to be one of those days,' sighed the man sitting behind me.

'What's that you just said?' asked DS Plank in a loud voice.

'I didn't say a word,' I replied.

'It was Mr Sleet-Street-Street's solicitor who coughed this time, sir,' Kennelly answered the detective sergeant.

DS Plank glared at me. 'Just you watch it, mate. I've got my eye on you. You've got a very suspicious foreigner's name. Aye, where are you from? Speak up, man ... do you need an interpreter?'

His eye, I wonder which one, I thought to myself. The real one or the one, which looked as if it was made of glass. It was a pity he hadn't got his ears turned on as well.

After a tediously long time and a lot of fiddling, the Plank bloke managed to get the tape machine working.

'Right, now where was I? Ah yes. Hello, hello, hello, what's all this, then? Come in Mr Sleet-Street-Street, take a seat,' shouted Sergeant Plank.

'Sorry to interrupt, Sarge but you have already invited the suspect in, and you have already introduced both yourself and me,' said DC Kennelly.

'Have, I? Well, we had better get started then, hadn't we? I'm bloody parched ... who do you have to shag to get a cup of tea around here? Right, here we go ... those who are also present in the room, speak your names, please.'

'Oh ... er ... yes, Mr Terence Nobsworth of On The Ball Solicitors. The Crown's appointed solicitor for Mr Sleet-Street-Street.'

'On the ball? That's a bloody stupid name. Whose idea was that, then and who do you work for? Speak up, man,' demanded the deaf DS Plank. 'And who the hell are you?' he shouted, pointing to someone, a woman as it turned out, who was standing in the shadows in a corner of the room.

'Who me?' she queried.

'Yes, you madam. Who are you?'

''Missus Lily Mingin, wot works here,' she replied.

'Oh, now do you just? So, tell me then, do you know this foreigner bloke here? Are you in on this foul murder ... are you his accomplice? Come on woman, speak up, has the cat suddenly got your tongue ... I bet it has. You could get hanged for this; this is a foul business, so it is,' said DS Plant, rubbing his chin.

'Sorry to interrupt again, Sarge,' said DC Kennelly. 'Mrs Mingin is the tea lady, she has just brought you a cup of tea.'

Poor woman, what followed must have been sheer agony for her. I had to sit there for over an hour while the woman was made to fill out a statement form, giving her reasons why she had only put one spoonful of sugar in DS Plank's tea, despite him ordering two.

'Have you anything to say madam as to why you should not be charged? Come on, speak up,' shouted Plank, frightening the poor woman.

'I'm a good girl, I am,' was all Mrs Mingin managed to say.

'Get out of here you cocky little madam and don't come back to Clacton again or you will be nicked.'

'We are in Skegness, Sarge ... not Clacton,' said DC Kennelly, looking quite exasperated.

'Oh yes. Well, make sure I don't see you, or the likes of you, around here ever again. They've got a good name and that's how they like it, and want to keep it.'

What followed was hour upon hour of interrogation. At some stage, sandwiches were brought in, and numerous cups of tea were drunk. God only knows how many cigarettes were smoked.

'No cement? what do you mean, no cement? This is not a bloody building site. The bloke's a bloody loony.'

'Sorry Sarge,' interrupted DC Kennelly. 'I think

you'll find that Mr Sleet-Street-Street actually said ... no comment.'

'Did he now. And are you, by any chance, trying to frustrate the workings of the law? Get out of here, man. You will be hearing from our solicitors in due course. Take him down, Kennedy,' DS Plant barked.

'It's Kennelly, Sarge.'

'Kennelly ... so you've changed your bloody name now, have you? An alias is it?' bawled the deaf Plank.

'Sorry Sarge. I'm Kennelly, he is Mr Sleet-Street-Street,' replied the detective constable.

'Kennelly? Who the hell is he? Never heard of him.'

I was glad to get out of that interview room. As I pulled the door shut, I heard DS Plank scream, *"next"*, and followed shortly by, *"Sobbing are you madam. Regret is it, got something to hide, have we?"*. As I made my way towards the exit, I passed the other forty-seven fellow holidaymakers who, along with myself, were suspects in the disappearance of Kevin Hiscock, the erstwhile manager of *The Loss Vagas Extra Hotel*, near Skegness.

With both fear and trepidation, I waited at the bottom of the steps leading up to the police station entrance, for news of Mary and our friends, Alan, Rose, Mick and Chris. Had Alan's reference to *murdering a bacon sarnie*, actually been a coded reference meaning *strangling the little bastard*. I had never smoked a cigarette in my entire life but at that moment, I thought about taking up the habit. I remembered, suddenly, something I had read about their calming influence.

I thought of the two ladies, who had squatted too close to some brambles and stinging nettles during an uncomfortable toilet stop on the coach journey, and an offer to borrow one, or even both, of Kevin's healing hands when we reached his hotel, which had been firmly rejected. *"Are you sure ladies? There are not many things, which are free these days, you know"*, I had heard him ask. *"I could kill that pervert, I could. My Reg would do the same, if he was still alive"*, one of the ladies was heard to say.

And, there was Mick. I remember him saying that he would like to shove the Carpenter's CD up his... Up his what? Up his own, or up Kevin's, I wondered. I thought of the sobbing Shirley, who had lost her mum, and needed just the one number, number twenty, to win the jackpot in the bingo, and her husband, Barry who had, at some stage, threatened to kill Kevin for disappointing her. I thought back to the night of Magic, to a man called, Fred, who had offered to go out and buy a sword and teach the Great Whodeani how to swallow it.

In fact, I felt sorry for all those who had threatened to do the same, including my lovely wife, Mary. She had screamed that she would like to get her hands on him, and her threat to *knee him in the bollocks*, must be coming back to haunt her.

I had noticed the man with the socially irresponsible and unacceptable comb-over appeared to be shaking and sweating profusely, as was the fat man in the equally unacceptable socks and sandals, who when challenged by Kevin, had replied that his reason was something Kevin could not possibly understand; it was called fashion, and to which Kevin had said - *"really"* . I ask you, what an insult.

The small puddle of water, which I had noticed under the feet of the little old lady, who had been glad of taking extra precautions by inserting another pad but, I wondered, did she now regret screaming that she wanted to *"scratch Kevin's bleedin eyes out"*? And there were all the women, who had sat in the front row, during the last night's riotous entertainment - the demonstration by Mr Bert Entwhistle, on how to strip the paint from the four coloured doors, but never got beyond the green door before being mobbed. I had asked him afterwards where he bought his stripper from. The poor man, he was so upset at losing his cap that he was unable to tell me. Maybe I might have a word with him after his interrogation. You never know, he could give me some useful tips.

I thought of Chris and the threat she had made with a melon, and poor Rose who, as it happens, had turned out to be somewhat of a sadist and had threatened to do the same but with a pineapple - ouch. Then there was the refined man, still looking refined I might say, who had threatened to end Kevin's life before dinner. And the chap who had issued a mortal threat at Mablethorpe, after complaining he was unable to find the open-air market and had shouted to Kevin, *"On which edge of the town was it, you tosser?"*

Now, all of a sudden, the extra charges, which Kevin had demanded for the serviettes, the use of a magnifying glass, toilet rolls, the exorbitant alcohol prices and taxi fares, seemed reasonable and fair. Everyone was agreeing that *The Loss Vagas Hotel Extra* was the finest hotel they'd had the good fortune to stay in.

People were trying to deflect suspicion away from themselves by turning to each other and saying how pleasant and kind they had thought Kevin Hiscock and his beautiful, but still moustachioed, wife had been. The sobbing Shirley, her husband Brian, and the man with the socially unacceptable comb-over, were telling all and sundry how nice Kevin and his wife were, and they had been added to their Christmas card lists.

'We have formed an everlasting friendship,' Shirley informed everyone. 'We've invited them both to come and see my husband's dinky toys and ferret collection, and Barry will even let Kevin help with the cleaning out of the cages.'

As I was sitting there on the small wall in front of the police station, a coach suddenly pulled up and parked in the large car park directly opposite. I did not take much notice at first, and I cannot explain why I looked up, but I did, and immediately broke into a cold sweat. Walking towards me was the man who had driven us all the way to Skegness and back. The man whose hat I had tossed out of a vent in the coach window. The man who had heard everything that had gone on while ferrying us all on holiday. He had heard all the threats, which had been made on the life of mine host, Mr Kevin Hiscock.

Our eyes met, and I smiled while he scowled. I said hello but he just wagged a finger as he walked past and climbed the steps, where he was met at the door by a police officer going in the same direction. The police officer asked him what his business was to which our driver replied.

'I have come here today to see my brother-in-law, Detective Sergeant Plank. I have some information for him, which might be of interest and enable him to solve the mystery surrounding the disappearance of a very good friend of mine, a bloke by the name of Kevin Hiscock. He owns a five-star hotel near here."

'Oh right ... okay ... please step this way sir,' said the police officer as he held open the door.

Chapter 25

Everything seemed pleasant through the softness of the haze of time. Even past sadness seemed sweet. It was the light, not the darkness, that I saw when I looked back. There were no shadows cast on the past. The roads that Alan and Rose, Mick and Chris, and Mary and myself had once travelled were now stretched out behind us. There were no sharp stones.

We had once lingered on the roses by the side of the road, not the brambles and nettles, which had once stung us. They were nothing but gentle cirrus waving in the breeze. The ever-growing chain of memory had only pleasant bonds, and the bitterness and sorrow of today were smiles the following day.

Those days are long gone, and I had no wish to waste my life thinking about what could have been and forgetting the potential that awaited me. If I sat back and regretted the chances I had missed, then opportunity would have flown away.

However, the things that I had long forgotten were not forgotten by others. Many miles away in Norwich a coroner, a jury, and an avenger of blood were meeting. They had gathered together in a courtroom, which was full of those who had a personal interest in the proceedings, but in which they had taken no part themselves.

It was just another normal, very ordinary day, and I was busy popping around the house with the hoover when I heard a rattle. Turning off the machine, I investigated, and yes, it was a eureka moment. I was so relieved and excited, and Mary would be the same, I thought to myself.

'Mary, I've found that earring stopper you lost all those weeks ago,' I shouted to her.

'Whatever,' she shouted back. 'Put the kettle on, will you, I've got my hands full at the moment. I'm sorting out my knickers drawer. Don't forget ... in a china cup, please.'

I was in the process of making my lovely long suffering wife a cup of tea, in a Stechcol fine bone china made exclusively for Heath McCabe England Dishwasher proof cup, when the telephone rang. I had a sort of premonition, thinking that this time it could be someone other than the Amazon lady at the other end of the line. I decided to grab the telephone before Mary had the chance to snatch it up and tell whoever it was on the other end to sod off. How glad I was that I did what I did. The call was from Mick. However, before I could get to say hello, his voice cut in.

'Phil, it's Mick. Turn the telly on, mate ... the BBC. There's a report about that hotel bloke, who went missing in Skegness. You remember, we stopped at his hotel. Well ... they've found a body.'

I was taken aback. I had erased the horrors of our

trip away together. The sliced bread for breakfast, the trip to a sandbank on the East Coast, and the near death experience during a live performance given by a geriatric stripper. Now the horrors came flooding back, and my hands were shaking.

'Cheers, mate. Speak to you later,' I replied as I almost dropped the handset down in its cradle.

'Quick, Mary,' I shouted. 'Turn the box on....' but before I could finish what I was going to say, she shouted back at me that she was already watching what Mick had phoned about. We just couldn't believe what we were seeing and hearing....

"Over now to our legal correspondent, Laura Goonsberg, who is outside Norwich Crown Court.

Thank you, Sophie... Today, despite Brexit, Mr Justice John Stretton, recorded a verdict of suicide in the case of Mr Kevin Hiscock, the manager of the world-famous Loss Vagas Hotel Extra, a popular five-star hotel on the outskirts of Skegness in Lincolnshire.

Mr Hiscock's body was discovered hanging upside down by his feet, and with his hands tied firmly behind his back, from Skegness's memorial clock, three months after he had disappeared. Witnesses have described that on the night of Mr Hiscock's disappearance there was chaos following an evening of rowdy entertainment in his hotel.

The coroner's report makes for grim reading. He said that Mr Hiscock had suffered a number of injuries, 49 penetrating wounds to be precise, any one of which, could have proved fatal, and in his opinion, they had been self-inflicted.

On examining the deceased's body, the coroner said

that he had also discovered a peaked hat, which had been wedged six inches up the deceased's anal passage. In addition, some bingo cards, with the number 'twenty' pencilled in on them, were found stuffed into his mouth, and an attempt had been made to scratch out his eyes.

Further, the soles of Mr Hiscock's feet appeared to have been burned by something, which the coroner described as being similar to a decorator's blow torch. He told the Court and the journalists who were present at the inquest, that he himself, had used a blow torch in the past, whilst decorating his house, and had recognised similar marks on the feet of his next door neighbour, whose house he had accidentally burned to the ground during these decorations, which he had been carrying out himself at the time.

A police spokesman, Detective Sergeant Plank, told the court extensive searches for Mr Kevin Hiscock had been carried out by members of his force and that Mr Hiscock's body had only been discovered when the town's Christmas decorations were being removed by local council workmen.

One of the workmen, Mr Albert Gobsworth described how he had discovered the body purely by chance, after he had been attending to a call of nature. He told members of the jury - "I were tekkin a piss whale t'coast were clear when I saw this bloke angin".

The owner of a Santa hat, which police believe was not the property of the deceased, is still being sought, and any information concerning the owner of this hat will be treated in the strictest confidence.

DS Plank would also like to get in touch with the owner of a length of rope, and a flat cap, which was also found at the scene, and the police are asking anyone who may have any information to come forward.

Mr Hiscock's wife, Eva, is being comforted by a close friend of the deceased, a Mr Jock Strapp - Skeggies celebrated and world-reknowned Pricker, waxing extra - a local tattoo artist.

Now back to you in the studio, Sophie....

Thank you, Laura. Were there any witnesses to the events leading up to the disappearance of Mr Hiscock?

Yes, Sophie there were. A Mr Reginald Entwhistle, who was employed by the hotel, to perform a stripping demonstration, told Mr Justice Stretton that on the night of Mr Hiscock's disappearance all was chaos. He told of what he called, "a reet load of mad women wot were charging t'stage tryin to grab is tool and shoutin, blow job, we'll give thee a bloody blow job". After this Mr Entwhistle told the Court that he did not remember anything else other than that he had been searching for his peaked cap up until now.

Thank you Laura.... Now on to the other news... Boris Johnson has been caught with his hand..."

'For Christ's sake, Mary, turn the bloody tv off ... we've heard enough!'

'Well, well, well, what a relief. The silly bugger did himself in then, didn't he?' said Mary, grinning.

'Yes,' I replied. 'So, it was all just a storm in a tea cup really. But ... I still haven't had an answer to my question.'

'And what question was that, dear?'

'How did you know this Hiscock bloke had a big knob?'

"I have added a big knob to your shopping list..."

'Alexa, for God's sake, STOP!'

DISCOVER PHIL'S

Days Out : Trilogy

Follow the exploits of The Funboy3 - Phil Street, his brother Ian (Bro) and their old school friend Alan Day (the Captain). Now and again, accompanied by their adopted Brummie friend, Michael Sweeney.

Join them on a light-hearted and amusing journey around the Midlands, visiting some of their favourite towns and watering holes.

This book is essential reading for those with a good sense of humour and for anyone interested in a pint and a plate of good honest pub grub.

Book 1 – A Catalogue of Ridiculous Yarns

Book 2 - More Ridiculous Yarns

Book 3 - Final Catalogue of Ridiculous Yarns

Available Now

FUNBOY3 SERIES

The Antidote Series

Follow the exploits of The Funboy3 - Phil Street, his brother Ian (Bro) and their old school friend, Alan Day (the Captain). Accompanied, more often than not, by their adopted Brummie friend, Michael Sweeney.

Join them once more on a light-hearted and amusing journey around the Midlands, visiting their favourite towns and watering holes.

This first book in the new Antidote series is essential reading for those with a good sense of fun and humour.......

Book 1 - The Antidote to BREXIT Boredom

Book 2 - The Antidote to Sense & Insensitivity

Available Now

Book 3 - The Antidote to Normality

Coming Soon

Printed in Great Britain
by Amazon